THE CURSE OF CRAIGIBURN

THE CURSE OF CRAIGIBURN

by

J. LARCOMBE REES

VICTORY PRESS
LONDON and EASTBOURNE

Reprinted 1975

ISBN 0 85476 116 0

Printed in Great Britain for
VICTORY PRESS (Evangelical Publishers Ltd.),
Lottbridge Drove, Eastbourne, Sussex,
by Fletcher & Son Ltd, Norwich

CHAPTER ONE

THE DISASTERS OF CRAIGIBURN

Father had said the house was cursed.

James surveyed it from the bare branches of the apple tree where he sat. Of course, now that he was older he realised that Father had meant the family and the people living in the house, but this afternoon the house itself looked cursed. The grey granite of the walls stood out harshly against the lighter grey of the sky, and the wind beat the branches of the pine trees relentlessly against the slate of the roof. The paint that Great Grandfather had put on the window-frames and the front door was peeling now, and Great Grandmother's heavy Victorian curtains were drawn tightly across the windows, while the garden which she had loved and cultivated had turned to a frightening wilderness.

Certainly, the house looked cursed.

It seemed to James, sitting in the apple tree, that all his life long he had lived under the shadow of the disasters that had happened in that farmhouse; and yet for so long he had not even been allowed to know what those disasters had been. That was the worst part of it all—no one would ever tell him.

"You'll know when you're older," they said when he asked. That had made the disasters grow in his mind, until he imagined such terrible things that he had to sleep with the blankets and sheets pulled over his head.

"It's only a few months ago that I really found out about it all," he whispered to himself, "yet it seems like years." He pushed his mind back to what now seemed the most important afternoon of his life. How it had rained that afternoon! He had dashed into Micklethwaite's with a shopping list as long as his arm. Mr. Micklethwaite kept the only shop in the district, but he sold everything that anyone could ever want—or he said he did. James grinned when he thought of Mr. Micklethwaite. He was so fat that some people said he never left his shop because he could not squeeze through the door. If you caught him in the right mood he could tell a story like no one else in Scotland; the only trouble was that his stories were usually about the misfortunes of other people in the district, and they were always true. James supposed that was why grown-up people never liked him, and why young people always did.

On this particular afternoon, James had discovered him sitting behind the counter, eating biscuits steadily. Now this was a very good sign—it meant that he was not busy that afternoon and that he felt in a story-telling mood.

"Goodness!" he exclaimed, as James walked into the shop. "You're the living image of your mother, standing there in the half light."

All the time that Mr. Micklethwaite was putting together the groceries from James' list (still munching happily at his biscuits) James had been thinking madly. This was the first time in his life that anyone had really mentioned his mother to him.

"If only I can start him talking, I might discover ... everything," he thought wildly. "If only no one will come into the shop and disturb us now." His heart had been beating painfully hard as he said, as casually as he could:

"Did you know my mother, then, Mr. Micklethwaite?"

"Know her?" he replied, swinging round from the shelf with his arm still in the air. "'Course I knew her; knew them all up there at the farm."

James swallowed hard. "Then you know about the disasters?"

"Know about them?" Mr. Micklethwaite said again. "'Course I know about them."

"Well, I don't yet," said James, very quietly; "don't you think I'm old enough now to know?"

Mr. Micklethwaite took a large chocolate biscuit and munched in silence. James remembered how he had waited for the answer to his question in the darkness of the little shop, and it had seemed as if Mr. Micklethwaite was eating the biggest biscuit in the world, so long did he take to chew it. Then at last he had said, in his rich Scottish voice:

"Maybe ye are old enough, James laddie, maybe ye are; but never let your father know I told you.

"I remember your old great grandmother well—a fine old lady, with a nose like an eagle's beak."

"I know," laughed James; "there's an old, brown

photograph of her in a big, black frame in the parlour. She's reading an enormous, great book."

"Aye," said Mr. Micklethwaite, "that would be her Bible. She would sit in her rocking-chair in the corner of the kitchen and read it by the hour. Some folks said she wasted too much time on it, but if they were in trouble those same folks would go straight to her for help. When I first opened the shop here, your father was a young man, working the farm with his father and mother, and the old lady lived with them, too. They were prosperous then, aye, they were prosperous. I could send only the best quality groceries up to Craigiburn Farm in those days."

"But what happened?" whispered James urgently.

"Well, your father's mother and father were out in the buggy one day, riding through the Forestry, they were, on the top ride, over the old quarry. The police said the horse must have been startled by a rabbit or something. Anyway, she bolted, and the buggy overturned them both into the quarry.

"Your poor father, just a young man. 'Never mind,' we all said, 'he's got the old lady; she'll take care of him.' That she did! She got up from her rocking-chair, put on her apron, and cooked, and cleaned and fussed him, but it was all too much for her at eighty-five, and she died within the year."

"So he was all on his own then."

"Aye, all on his own, with a farm to manage, and him only just passed his twenty-first birthday. He would not sell the farm, against all our advice, and carried on with only Mr. McQueen and that old rascal Dougal to help him; but he lost all his pigs with the swine fever one year, and most of his harvest with fire, the next. I don't know how he ever managed, for he had nothing but disaster after disaster. It would have been no wonder if ne had gone to the bad and run off like his Uncle Harry, the black sheep of the family."

Mr. Micklethwaite was heartily enjoying himself now, as he always did when he told a depressing story.

"Of course, we were all glad when we saw him courting your mother. He would have been about twenty-eight then."

This was the heart of the story; it was for this that Jamie seemed to have been waiting all his life. He held his breath and thought, "If anyone comes into the shop now, I don't know what I'll do."

"What was she like?" he asked by way of encouragement.

"Oh, she'd long, golden hair—the colour of yours —which she never tied back or covered with a hat. She was a wild girl, that one, always laughing and enjoying every minute of her life; but she was never so happy as when she was across the back of her horse, riding madcap all over the countryside. She had a great, black beast, as spirited as she was—I always said from the beginning that horse was not safe. They were married in the winter, and you were born a year later."

There was a long, uncomfortable silence in the shop. At last James said in a tiny voice, quite unlike his own:

"I suppose I was one of the disasters, myself."

"Aye, Laddie, you were. There were those that said it was a judgment on your mother for her wild ways, but the doctors at the infirmary said it was just one of those things that happen. At first they said you might never speak or understand what went on round you. Be thankful, Jamie, that you are all right in your head, even if some of the rest of you is not what it should be. Aye, be thankful for that."

James remembered looking down at the great boot with the special thick sole, at the end of his thin left leg, and his clumsy left arm and hand, and feeling bitterly that there was not much for which to be thankful. A terrible thought had struck him then.

"Did my father mind much . . . about me, I mean?"

Mr. Micklethwaite took another biscuit to cover the awkwardness.

"When a farm has been in a man's family for many years, he likes to have a strong son to keep up the tradition after him; but your mother laughed him out of the sadness and said they would have many other sons. Then off she went, riding that great, black horse, day after day, and you a tiny, sickly baby, no more than a few months old.

"Aye, but it came to an end. How I remember that terrible day! She came riding by the shop here and waved to me as she went towards the hills. I never saw her again. As soon as I heard the news I went up to the farm." Mr. Micklethwaite never could resist a drama.

"Dr. Carter said if they had only taken her straight

to the infirmary in Newton Castle there might have been some hope, but they took her home to the house when they found her lying in the heather. No one could find the horse for three days.

"Dougal and I sat in the kitchen all that evening and made tea. What a night that was; I have never known a wind like it. It beat itself against the walls of the house and moaned in the chimney."

James thought he would always remember the way Mr. Micklethwaite's face had come nearer and nearer to him as he leant across the counter, enjoying each word of the story he told.

"Aye, it was a terrible night. At last the boards creaked overhead, and Dr. Carter came down and went straight out. After a time your father came slowly into the kitchen and shut the door and leant his back against it.

" 'It's no good', he said, 'I know for certain now God is against me. Once I loved Him, now I hate Him, so I'll shut Him out of my house, and out of my life, and out of my son's life, too. I'll have nothing more to do with Him. This house is cursed.'

"Well, then something seemed to possess him, and he went from room to room, tearing from the walls the texts that your great grandmother had put there, and as he left each room the wind slammed the door shut after him so that the whole house seemed to shake. Then he took her great Bible from the shelf, and with the wall texts he burnt it on a bonfire in the yard. After that he went into the house, leaving us outside, and the wind slammed the back door after him, just as if God really was shut out of the house for ever."

"What happened then?" James whispered.

"Why, the wind took the flames of the fire towards the hay barn, and, if we hadn't been there to beat them out, the whole yard would have been ablaze in no time."

"Was the Bible burnt right up?"

"No, not quite. I told Dougal to finish it off on the kitchen fire, but he said he had too much respect for the old lady to do that, so he hid it somewhere, I can't remember where, and neither can he, I doubt."

James shivered and turned up his coat collar; it was cold in the apple tree. What an afternoon that had been, but what an unexpected ending it had had. Poor Mr. Micklethwaite! He loved to tell a good story and to build up the tension until he sent his hearers shaking from the shop; but that afternoon his enjoyment had been spoilt and his sense of drama bitterly hurt. He had become so excited as he reached the climax of his tale, that he had swallowed two biscuits at once. His eyes began to water, his face turned purple and he had had to retire into his bedroom behind the shop, coughing, sneezing and choking all at once. James had gone out of the shop shaking all right, not with fear but with laughter, and he had laughed all the way home. He felt most ashamed of laughing after having heard about the terrible disasters, but if he had not laughed he would have cried, which would have shamed him even more.

He climbed awkwardly down from the apple tree,

still grinning at the thought of Mr. Micklethwaite's streaming eyes, but he vowed as he did so, as he had vowed a thousand times before, that he would find that Bible or die in the attempt.

CHAPTER TWO

THE UGLY MAN OF THE FOREST

James shut the back door firmly on the raw winter afternoon, and a thrill of warm pleasure went through him as he looked round the old-fashioned kitchen, with its red-tiled floor, solid wooden table and great open fire. This was home. Craigiburn might look harsh and forbidding from the outside, but once you stepped into the kitchen everything combined to welcome you.

He shrugged himself out of his mack with difficulty, hung it on one of the pegs which the men of his family had used for generations and smiled to himself as he saw Aunt Hester's black one beside it. Father and he never said anything to each other about it, but they never moved that mackintosh, because whenever they looked at it they felt a feeling of secret pleasure that Aunt Hester would never be coming back to wear it again.

Aunt Hester (who was no one's proper aunt) had 'taken charge' of James, his father and the house after the last disaster, and James, his father and the house had never got over the misery of her. She cleaned everything and everybody from morning until night, fussing, nagging and scolding as she went.

They lived in a great state in all the rooms of the

14

house then, except the kitchen, and they were never allowed in there because it was Aunt Hester's private Kingdom, in which she made horrible fish pies and rice puddings, and washed clothes long before they were dirty.

James remembered the fierce, prickling anger that he had felt that day, two years ago, when as usual she would help him to take off his coat and outdoor shoes after school.

"I may not be very strong," he had said through his teeth, "but I'm not a cissy!"

Father had heard him, and suddenly something had seemed to explode inside his usually quiet self, and he had banged his fist down on the table and said, "That's just what you're doing; you're turning my son into a helpless invalid, and my house into a museum of ... of ... cleanliness." And he had said a great many other, most enjoyable things, which James had longed to say for years.

By the end of the day she was gone, but she took her revenge by leaving a dreadful fish pie in the oven for their tea.

James began to set the table, using his strong right hand to compensate for the clumsiness of his left. What bliss life had been ever since! He and Father had shut up all the rooms in the house, and they lived happily together in the kitchen and the two servants' bedrooms above it.

James filled the kettle and put it on the stove. Aunt Hester would never have let him do a thing like that. It was wonderful to be treated like a man and not like a baby. He crouched down and looked into the oven, and he nearly fell over backwards with delight. Mrs. McQueen had left a steak and kidney pie today. Mrs. McQueen 'came in' each afternoon; she was very fat and had nine children and no teeth. She hated cleaning but always cooked something delicious for their tea.

Suddenly something hurled itself at the back door, and all at once the kitchen was full of the two great sheep-dogs, hungry for their food, and Father hungry for his. Soon all four of them were eating in silent enjoyment. James and his father never bothered to speak to each other, unless it was necessary; they just enjoyed each other's company in silence—chattering was for women, and there was no woman in that house now to disturb a man's peace with remarks about elbows on the table. Unfortunately, neither was there a woman to clear away the dishes, but that was soon done, and Father arranged himself at one end of the table with the farm accounts, while James sat at the other with his homework. The dogs groaned with pleasure on the hearthrug, and the fire stained the peaceful walls of the kitchen a deep, rich red.

School would be lovely, if it wasn't for that playground, thought James as he walked through the forest next morning. Everyone was equal sitting behind their desks in the one big room that was the village school. But as soon as break or lunch hour arrived and someone said, "Let's play *He*!", things were not equal any more, and it was not much fun, turning your back on the game and pretending you enjoyed throwing pebbles at a tin can in the corner.

Anyway, he thought, it's Saturday tomorrow.

Something rustled suddenly among the forest trees that he was passing. He stopped abruptly and swung round, straining his eyes and ears. An evil-looking stoat rushed across the path and disappeared into the bracken and feather grass, then all was silent once again. It was wonderful to walk to school through the forest, for you never knew what you would see among the dark rows of trees.

The forest was a large one, stretching over many acres of the countryside. There was a great mystery about who owned it now, for no one knew, except the Forest Manager who was in charge of the men and trees, but he would never say who employed him, however much he was questioned.

James loved every one of the tall, straight larch and Scots pine, but the forest was sometimes a frightening place to be alone in. He was out of it now, however, and the village lay below him. He could see Mr. Micklethwaite's shop; the kirk and the manse; the school, surrounded by the grey playground, and the white Golf Hotel, with the golf-course stretching away behind it, merging into the dark green wall of the forest.

The path was steep here, and James took it slowly. He was half-way down, when from behind him came a noise like a herd of wild cattle stampeding. Stones rattled angrily in all directions, and some startled rooks flew up, squawking with fear. Round the corner, at full tilt, came a giant of a boy, with his great, black boots pounding on the path and his satchel flying out like a rudder behind him. He came to a marvellous skier's halt beside James, and grinned.

"Man, I thought I was late for school again," he panted. "I've been up half the night, helping with the lambing."

Rory was so passionately fond of farming that he could talk of little else, and he always went to bed with a large book on agriculture under his pillow.

"If only I was strong like Rory," thought James as they walked on together, "my father would be so proud of me."

Rory talked on happily about twin lambs until they reached the Golf Hotel, where Gordon was waiting for them. His father owned this little place, but to hear Gordon talk you would think he lived in the Grand Hotel, Edinburgh, instead of the small house where the unfortunate guests had to bear his mother's terrible cooking and his father's boring 'funny' stories.

Gordon had on a brand-new waistcoat that morning, and as he stood waiting for them he had arranged his jacket to show it off to the full.

"Hullo, you two," he said, rather as a king might address two tramps. "Do you know what I'm going to do tomorrow morning?"

"Have your breakfast?" said James sourly.

Gordon eyed him witheringly. "No, after breakfast. I have been asked to caddy for Sir Humphrey Mace when he plays golf with the Professional. They told him I was the finest caddy in the district. He's staying with us, you know." He said it as though people with titles were as common in the hotel as cheese.

The three of them walked towards school, with Rory talking about his farm on one side, Gordon talking about his own cleverness on the other and James in the middle, wishing their height did not make him feel so small.

It was the last lesson of the afternoon, and it was history for the three top classes. There were twenty-eight children in the school, and only one teacher. They all worked together in one room, but each class sat in a separate row. James sat at the back in the top class, with Rory, Gordon and the others. They had to work very hard there because, as Miss Clark, the teacher, often said with a jangle of her many silver bracelets, "We do want you all to get to the Academy in Newton Castle."

James noticed that when she said that her eyes always fell disparagingly upon Sebastian. James sat next to him and, like everyone else, considered him rather a stupid kind of boy, but he could not help liking him, all the same. His ears stuck out from his head, and he always wore big, flappy corduroy shorts, and shoes with elastic sides. He was sitting now, thinking of nothing whatever, with his mouth open. Rory was on the other side of James, busily drawing a plan for a new style of sheep-dip on the back of his history book.

Suddenly a note was passed along the back row, from Gordon. "Let's all go to Micklethwaite's for ice lollies after school," it said. Now no one except Gordon ever had any pocket money left by Friday, but everyone always did what Gordon wanted to do because it was so much safer.

The whole top class walked along the road together: Rory, Sebastian, James, Gordon and the Ferguson twins, who were the daughters of the Forest Manager. The twins were very much alike, but yet quite different. Their mother made them dress exactly the same, but Violet looked as neat as a fashion model in her clothes, while Heather always looked like a scarecrow.

Heather was wildly enthusiastic about anything that they were doing. "Come on," she shouted to the rest of them, "we may get a good story out of him today."

She dashed on, her school hat flying as she went, and, arriving first at the shop, she ran up the two steps and was about to go in when she froze, staring through the glass window in the door. Something about her made the others stop dead, too.

"Quick!" she hissed at them. "Round the back of the shop! It's the Ugly Man of the Forest, and he's just coming out."

They all dived behind the shop, but James was not quick enough, so he nearly collided with the ragged, old tramp, who most people said was the ugliest man in Scotland.

They all crouched together as they watched him hobble away towards the forest, with his sack of groceries on his back.

"Oh, my!" breathed Heather, "wouldn't it be awful to meet him on your own in the forest?"

They all crowded into the shop, feeling rather shaky about the knees.

"Did you see yon fellow?" asked Micklethwaite, reaching far into the deep freeze for Gordon's ice lolly. "When he comes into the shop, the hairs stand up on my head."

As Mr. Micklethwaite had no hair whatsoever, no one believed that statement, but they watched him with round eyes as he leant across the counter and said, "Old Gavin Campbell, the forester, was in here yesterday, and he told me that he was passing that place of his in the forest—it's only a caravan, you ken, with a fence all round it—but do you know what he heard?"

"What?" breathed everyone together, and James was sure his hair was standing up like Mr. Micklethwaite said his did.

"Aye, do you know what he heard coming from behind that high fence? Terrible noises—bumps and squeaks and strange chattering noises."

"Whatever do you suppose he has behind that fence?" said Sebastian, whose great ears had turned purple with excitement.

"No one can tell," replied Mr. Micklethwaite darkly, "because the fence is too high to see over. But I'm sure of one thing—he's up to no good. I have a cousin who has a shop next to the station in Newton Castle, and he told me he sees him often, walking to the station with a wheelbarrow full of small wooden boxes. He puts them on a train, and a few days later they come back to him again. But where those wooden boxes have been and what they contain, I tremble to think!"

Mr. Micklethwaite was so overcome by frustrated curiosity, that he had to have an ice lolly himself, and they left him licking it and brooding over the dark mystery.

"Oh, goodness," said Heather when they were outside, "I would give anything I possess to know what's behind that fence."

"So would I," said Sebastian, "but none of us would ever dare to take a look."

"Oh, I don't know about that," boasted Gordon loftily. "I wouldn't mind; it would be quite easy, really. Just sneak quietly up, put a ladder against the fence and—Bob's your uncle—you've seen everything. No, I shouldn't be at all afraid."

"Then why don't you do it tomorrow?" said Sebastian enthusiastically. "We'll all come with you."

"Yes," added Heather, "and we'll have a picnic tea in the forest; we won't be too cold."

"I ... er ... well, I'm busy tomorrow, caddying," replied Gordon, thankful for the excuse.

"But that's only in the morning," said Rory.

"Well, I haven't got a ladder," Gordon was getting desperate now.

"Oh, we have one of the new light-weight, folding kind," said Rory proudly. "Father will let me have it."

Gordon was cornered, and he knew it.

"Very well then," he said crossly, "but don't blame me if we're shot dead—or eaten by terrible squeaking, chattering beasties."

CHAPTER THREE

"SO I'VE GOT YOU!"

Next day after dinner they set off in winter sunshine. James did not usually go about with the others much, because he hated to feel that they had to wait for him and help him over gates and walls, but today he was too desperate with curiosity to care.

Rory carried the ladder and a huge haversack containing everyone's picnic tea. He was so strong that he would have carried twice the amount and never felt the weight.

They plunged straight into the forest, and soon the sombre darkness and rather frightening silence had engulfed them.

"Let's take the road by the Bottomless Loch,' said Gordon. He was in a very good mood that afternoon, because Sir Humphrey had given him seven and six-pence instead of the usual five shillings. So he decided to have a little fun by teasing Sebastian.

"Sebastian," he said, "do you know about the Bottomless Loch?"

"No," replied Sebastian, staring vacantly at Gordon with his mouth open.

"You mean your father never warned you about it?"

"No."

"Then you don't know about the monster."

Everyone else kept their faces very straight. Poor

Sebastian always believed everything that he was told, and rose beautifully to any bait.

"Well, Sebastian," Gordon continued, "you know the Loch Ness Monster? Well, he's only just a wee tadpole in comparison with this creature, and, what's more, this monster has been known to eat people alive."

"Don't you think we should go by the other road?" said Sebastian desperately; his ears were already turning purple.

"Maybe we should do that," Gordon replied, "but I like you, Sebastian, so I'll tell you what I'll do; I'll let you into the secret of the Monster. You only have to give it some food once, and it's like an elephant; it never forgets you, and you are safe for life. If I were you, I should throw it your picnic tea."

Sebastian's face was a study of dismay. "But I've got jam tarts," he said piteously.

"My dear Sebastian," said Gordon sadly, "what is a jam tart in comparison with your life?"

They had reached the loch by then, and Heather was hugging a pine tree in an agony of giggles, while Rory seemed to be having a coughing fit. Slowly and sadly Sebastian took the haversack from him and walked alone to the edge of the lake. There was a splash, and he returned looking much happier.

"It was worth it," he said; "I'm most grateful to you, Gordon; in fact, one good turn deserves another, so I threw in your picnic, too."

"You did what?" screamed Gordon, thinking of his favourite cheese and pickle sandwiches.

"I threw yours in, so you would be safe as well. Aren't you pleased?"

If it had not been for the fact that Gordon fell over the ladder on his way to Sebastian, that unfortunate individual might have joined his picnic in the loch.

They moved off again, with Gordon still rubbing his nose which he had banged in his fall, and the forest grew darker and more forbidding still.

"We had better keep our voices down," whispered Heather. "We must be getting near now."

Very soon they reached the clearing where the old man lived behind his fence. No one could think why the Forest Manager allowed him to live there, and Mr. Micklethwaite said it was a disgrace.

They all crept silently up to the fence—silently, that is, except Sebastian, whose big feet always seemed to step on the noisiest of twigs.   The moment had come. The ladder was unfolded and placed against the fence; everyone's heart was beating rapidly, and all wished they had never come.

"Up you go, Gordon," whispered Sebastian, tactless as ever.

"Oh," Gordon replied in a hoarse whisper, "did I forget to tell you? Doctor Carter said I must never climb a ladder. I suffer from verti-somethingorother."

"But you were all right yesterday, weren't you?" Heather whispered back anxiously.

"Oh, this came on quite suddenly this morning," said Gordon, trying to look as ill as he could.

Everyone was very crestfallen, and they all tiptoed back to the shelter of the trees to hold a council of war.

"Well, I'm much too scared to go," stated Rory, sitting down firmly on a tree-stump.

"It's no use sending Sebastian," added Gordon. "He's too stupid to tell us what he can see when he gets up there."

"I can't climb that filthy ladder; I might dirty my new skirt," said Violet primly.

"I'll go," said James into the silence which followed.

"You!" everyone said at once, looking at James in surprise. "*Can* you climb a ladder?"

James was not at all sure that he could, but he said, "Of course I can," very coldly, and set off for the fence.

His greatest fear in life was that they should think him a cissy, and here was a chance to show them that he was not one.

"If only I don't get stuck half-way up and make a fool of myself," he thought desperately.

When they arrived at the ladder he went up the first few rungs very slowly, with Sebastian holding it tightly at the bottom. It is very difficult to climb a ladder when only one leg is any use but, after much panting and struggling, he was at the top, and he had his right leg over and was sitting astride the fence so that he could balance better. However, before he had a chance to see anything, disaster struck in the form of Sebastian. So great was his excitement that he was jumping up and down, and the next minute one of his big feet knocked against the ladder. Suddenly everything seemed to happen at once. The ladder fell sideways with a terrible crash, leaving James clinging to the top of the fence, a loud and angry shouting came from somewhere below him, and he caught a glimpse of everyone dashing for the cover of the trees, with Sebastian falling over a tree-root and squealing like a slaughtered pig. Suddenly the hard ground came up and hit James on the shoulders, and he lay still.

At first he wondered if he was dead, because he seemed to be floating, and everything was swaying about him like seaweed in the ocean. At length he became aware of some rather dirty toes sticking out from the end of even dirtier boots. Above the toes was a ragged pair of trousers, and far above them all was the face of the ugliest man in Scotland.

"So I've got you!" he said in a voice like the cawing of a rook.

James swallowed hard and struggled to his feet, making towards the gate that he could see in the fence.

"I'm sorry I bothered you," he said. "I'm just going now."

"You've hurt your leg," stated the man without sympathy.

"Oh, no," James replied hurriedly, "I was born like that."

"Come into my caravan and take tea." It was a command, not an invitation.

"Oh, no, thank you, I must be on my way." James was desperate now.

"I said, come into my caravan and take tea."

There was no arguing now, so James followed him

inside. Afterwards, when the others asked him, he could never remember what the inside of the caravan was like, except that it was very dark and quite full of silver cups. They stood on the table, on the shelves and on the floor. Some were very big and others were tiny.

The man pushed him down on to a bench and began to pour tea out of a large, black teapot into enamel mugs, adding tinned milk and sugar from a packet, stirring everything round and round with a toothbrush.

James watched him as a rabbit watches a weasel. Was it possible that anyone could be that ugly? It was his nose. It was nearly black and spread all over his face in extraordinary directions. He had only three teeth, and they were yellow like an old dog's, and you really could not see where his shaggy hair ended and his beard began.

"I am ugly, aren't I?" The harsh voice cut across Jamie's horrified thoughts like a blow.

"I ... er ... I didn't mean ..." he stammered.

"That's just why I live here, far from anyone else; I can't bear being stared at." He looked sadly into his mug of tea. "All my life I worked among trees—in Canada mostly—trying to get away from people. I came here twenty years ago, when I retired, to shut myself away from them for ever, but I still can't stand being stared at."

Suddenly something in James seemed to go out to this man, and for the moment he forgot to be frightened.

"You know, that's just how I feel sometimes," he said impulsively. "I'm lame, you see."

"Aye," said the man, and he got up quickly and rinsed his mug in a bowl of cold water. Then he suddenly turned viciously on James, waving the dripping cup in the air.

"Boy!" he shouted hoarsely, "you must never be afraid of people, or you'll spoil your life. You came trespassing on my property, so you will listen to me now." There was not much chance of James doing otherwise, pinioned as he was against the wall of the caravan, with the battered mug waving not two inches from his nose.

"With people, attack is the best form of defence," shouted the old man. "If you're feeling miserable because of yourself and the way you look, remember that they are feeling miserable because of themselves, too. Maybe they're fat, or maybe they squint, or maybe they're not clever, or maybe they even have a nose like mine." His voice was getting louder and louder. "Look them straight in the eye, and remember they all feel silly about something."

Suddenly he collapsed in his chair, with his hand over his eyes.

"Someone once told me all that, and I tried all my life to do it, but I never could. You remember it, boy, or you'll become a lonely, old man like me."

Then he took his hand from his face and said in quite a different voice, "How would you like to own a champion?"

Now the only kind of champion that James'

harassed mind could conjure up at that minute was a boxing champion, and he wondered vaguely what Father would say if he took one home.

"Follow me," commanded the old man, "and I'll give you something to remind you of today."

James followed him laughing mirthlessly inside himself. He would not need anything more to remind him: he would never forget this nightmare.

They stepped out of the caravan and went behind it. For one minute James had the impression that he was in a vast city, with blocks of flats on either side of him. Then he realised they were not flats, but hutches, placed one upon another in tiers against the fence and the back of the caravan, and they were not walking down a street, but along a path between the hutches.

Each one contained guinea-pigs of all different sizes, and everyone of them, when they saw the man, stood up against the wire at the front of the cages and squeaked a welcome. The noise was tremendous.

"That's what old Gavin Campbell heard," thought Jamie, as he stared in fascination at the beautiful animals.

"These are some of the most famous cavies in the country," said the man with great pride. "No, these are not ordinary cavies."

"But I thought they were guinea-pigs," said James, rather confused.

"Oh, that's only their common name; those of us who breed champions call them cavies. I send them to great shows up and down the country. They have won all those silver cups in the caravan. I've won more prizes with them than anyone else in Great Britain."

"But how do they get to the shows, if you don't go with them?"

"Oh, breeders like me can't be trotting all over the country with their stock; no, we put them in little, wooden travelling boxes—like this one—and send them by train, and the show officials collect them."

"But don't the guinea-pigs mind?"

"Goodness no! I think they enjoy it. I give them a big meal of their favourite food before they go, and when they come back—having won all the prizes—they have an egg beaten up in milk. They are so proud of themselves, I think they know they are champions."

He looked at his little city fondly. "They don't mind my being ugly," he said, opening the door of a large cage. "This is The Emperor," he added with great pride, "the corner-stone of the strain. He's a treble champion. See these markings, white, tan and black; look how each is a perfect square, meeting in a line down his back, and look at that Roman nose and the way his ears fall. Perfect he is. Perfect."

All the other guinea-pigs in the other hutches were the same colour and had the same markings, but none looked as proud as The Emperor.

"Of course, I breed a great many cavies, but I keep only the very best. The wasters—the young ones that aren't quite perfect—I send to pet shops in England. I keep only a few of the finest for showing and breeding. See these?" He opened another hutch with six adorable babies, just the size of mice, inside it.

"See that one, the one scratching her ear? She'll be a champion some day, but the rest, well..." They passed on down the row.

Suddenly James found himself being regarded by a pair of sleepy, brown eyes, and, when a pink nose was twitched at him, he knew that he had completely lost his heart.

"Oh, what's this one's name?" he asked.

"That's Peter, The Emperor's grandson; he won his first show last week. You can have him."

"Have him?" repeated James dumbly. "Have him for myself?"

"I said I'd give you something to remind you of today, didn't I?" said the man crossly. "Here, you can take him in this old hutch. Just feed him a little bran and crushed oats each day, and plenty of green stuff, especially grass, when the spring comes. He'll do well, bless him!"

As he tied the hutch to Jamie's back, as one would wear a haversack, he asked, "What's your name, boy?" When James told him, there was a startled pause, and the old man stepped back against the fence, a look of horror on his face. "So you are a Brodie of Craigiburn," he said in a strange, tight voice. "You had best go at once and never come near me again." And the next minute James found himself outside, and the gate in the fence was slammed shut.

CHAPTER FOUR

AN UNCANNY MESSAGE FROM THE PAST

"Here you are, Peter; I've got you a lovely piece of cabbage."

James pushed it into the hutch, and Peter ran forward eagerly. He had a way of eating right at the front of his hutch, with his brown eyes fixed adoringly on James, while his sharp front teeth munched furiously.

He had settled down very quickly in his hutch in the little wooden hut known as the harness room. No one had used the room since Jamie's mother had saddled up her big, black horse for the last time eleven years before. It was still full of saddles and harness, and it smelt beautifully of leather and horses and linseed oil.

James sat on an upturned wooden bucket and watched Peter eat. It was Sunday afternoon, and there was nothing else to do. The day before had been so very exciting, that today reaction was making Jamie feel flat and bored.

"What a long, hungry, horrible day Sunday is," he said out loud, "and now it's beginning to rain."

Sundays always stretched before James in depressing endlessness, and he was usually chronically hungry, for Mrs. McQueen never came at week-ends,

and Father liked to lie in bed all day and got up only
to open a tin of baked beans for dinner, and they ate
stale baps with jam for tea.

It was a long, hungry day all right.

"Everyone else will be at Sabbath School now," he
thought. "I suppose they learn about God there,
lucky beasts!" he added with a sigh.

God was a complete mystery to James, because all
his life he had been prevented from discovering anything about Him. One of his earliest memories was of
his father saying to Aunt Hester, "Now remember,
Hester, I'll not have the boy taught anything about
God."

James had looked forward to starting school for the
only reason that he hoped he would find out about
God there; but Father had taken him in the Land-
Rover the first day and had had a long talk with Miss
Clark, who secretly agreed with Father about God. So
James always had to read a book in the cloakroom
during Scripture and Prayers, and, however much he
tried, he could never hear what went on, on the other
side of the well-fitting door.

His curiosity had grown as time went on, until one
day he asked Dougal, "Is God a thing or a person?"

Dougal had scratched the bald part of his head and
said he didn't rightly know. "But," he had added,
"there are those in these parts who say the wrath of
God will fall on your father, for bringing you up in
'ignorance' as he is." Dougal always said words the
wrong way round. "But the wrath of your father will

fall on me if I tells ye any more, so be off wi' you, and think on somethin' else."

James had tried to 'think on somethin' else', but this strange thing called God fascinated him. One day he had gone into the public library in Newton Castle —the nearest town—and dug about on the dusty shelves. He had learnt a bit about archaeology and a lot about basket-making, but nothing whatever about God. At last, one day, conquering his shyness, he had asked Violet. She had looked down her nose—as only Violet could—and said, "Well, James, if you are as ignorant as all that, I'm not going to tell you."

He had fared little better with Heather, for she was in one of her giggling moods when he asked her.

After that he felt too embarrassed to ask anyone else at school, but one afternoon he walked up and down outside the manse, trying to pluck up enough courage to ask the minister. But he was very old and very deaf, and in the end James could not face shouting his questions down his old-fashioned ear-trumpet, so he had gone home to tea. Now here he was, eleven years old and still consumed with curiosity.

He was also excessively cold. "I think I'll go in by the fire," he said to Peter, who was curled up in a cosy ball and took no notice of him. "Well, good-night," said James, rather grieved at his lack of interest; but Peter only curled into a tighter ball and sighed contentedly.

James hurried across the yard with his collar turned up against the cruel March wind which was howling down from the bare, craggy hills above the farm. As

he passed the wood-shed he remembered that Father
had asked him to bring in some logs, so he slipped
inside, and the smell of seasoned wood engulfed him.

Dougal always chopped wood when he was in a bad
temper, so the shed was usually bursting with logs,
but he had been in a very good mood for several
months, ever since Father had given him a rise, so
that day the little room was nearly empty.

James was poking about idly, looking for what he
wanted, when suddenly, right at the bottom of what
had once been a great pile of logs, his eye fell on
something that was certainly not a log of wood. James
squatted down and began to pull at the old sack
which was covering something large and square.

"It's some kind of a box!" he said, suddenly
breathless with excitement. "Maybe it's hidden
treasure, and we'll be able to go on a holiday to England or even buy a racing-car."

He started to tear furiously at the sacking, but it
was stiff and sticky with age. "Whatever's in here? It's
mighty heavy—could be gold coins or great big
jewels." The sack gave way at last, and the heavy
thing that it contained fell to the floor with a loud
thud.

At first disappointment spread through Jamie like
a pain. "It's only an old, burnt-up book," he said.
"But where have I seen it before?" Suddenly all
Jamie's disappointment had changed to unbelievable
excitement. He forgot about treasure and racing-cars;
he forgot about being hungry and cold; he had found
what he had been looking for for months—the thing

that had been lying hidden here ever since the terrible, windy night when Father had shut God out of his life. It looked sadly different from its picture in the parlour, but James recognised it easily by its brass covers and clasp—it was undoubtedly Great Grandmother's long-lost Bible.

For a full minute he sat among the logs and stared, afraid to touch it in case it disappeared by some magic. Then very slowly he opened the blackened cover, and there, carefully pasted inside, was a photograph of his great grandmother as a young girl, with long, black hair. Underneath in her old-fashioned handwriting she had written her name.

Suddenly James became rigid, gazing at the page, for he had seen his own name, written under his great grandmother's, and the strangest thing of all was that it had also been written by her.

> 'James 4, verse 8. [he read]
> Draw near to God, and He will draw
> near to you.'

"However did she know my name?" he wondered, "and what does the '4, verse 8' bit mean? Just fancy her writing me a message years before I was born! It's uncanny!"

He turned over the pages with trembling fingers; some of the leaves were so badly burnt they could not be read, but others were quite clear.

Suddenly a thought struck Jamie, blindingly. "Now, at last," he said to himself, "I shall be able to find out all I want to know about God." He stood up, hugging the Bible to himself, and wishing he could laugh and cry and scream and shout all at the same time.

"I'll take it to the harness room," he said, "and I'll read every word that I can, until I really know."

It was more than just curiosity now; as he hobbled across the yard he felt as if some great power had taken hold of him and was forcing him towards the knowledge which he craved.

Sitting down on his old bucket, he opened the old book and began to read. All at once the great words seemed to thunder out at him:

'In the beginning God created the heavens and the earth.'

He could see him doing it, too, for he always saw pictures of everything that he read about, and now it all seemed to be happening before him. He could see God rolling the world into a ball like plasticine and throwing it into space, forming the seas, and then drawing in the continents and islands—just as James himself drew them in geography. Then he watched the grass growing and the arrival of the 'fowls' and the 'great whales', and at last man himself.

"Goodness!" gulped James, his eyes round with wonder. "God must be strong. Why on earth did Great Grandmother tell me to draw near to Him? I could never possibly draw near to anyone as mighty as all that. Why! He couldn't even know that I exist."

He read on, hardly able to turn the pages for excitement. He had just arrived at the place where the serpent was talking to Eve, and he had his fingers crossed in an agony of fear, trying to stop her taking the forbidden fruit, when he heard Father calling him for tea.

Guiltily he hid the Bible under the bucket and hurried in to spend an anxious evening sitting on the edge of Great Grandmother's rocking-chair, hoping Father would not ask why he was so restless. Fortunately, Father was, as usual, so occupied with his farming magazines that he noticed nothing.

The next morning, as soon as breakfast was finished, James made a dash for the harness room, but by the time he had fed Peter, and seen Adam and Eve turned out of the garden, he realised he would be very late for school.

He ran all the way, as fast as his lame leg would let him, and arrived at the door, hot and panting.

"Horrors!" he said, as he heard the sound of multiplication tables being chanted from inside, "I must be late, they're doing arithmetic already!" He opened the door and slipped inside.

People usually did look at you a bit when you were late, but today it was dreadful. There was a sudden, electrified silence in the room, then everyone stood up and stared. Pencils and books dropped to the floor, and some of the little ones dropped their counting frames.

"Well," said Miss Clark, taking off her glasses, "after what I have heard of your adventures on Saturday, I hardly expected to see you in school at all today."

Everyone went on with their work, but they kept looking at James as if he had been King Robert the Bruce come back from the dead. Heather told him later that Gordon had had a wonderful time going round telling everyone how he had bravely gone back to rescue James, but he had heard such screams and groans and sounds of torture that he had had to go away again. "Of course, I knew jolly well it wasn't true, but everyone else believed him," finished Heather with a giggle.

As soon as break came, James found himself in the playground, surrounded by the whole school, all talking at once and asking him questions. He could not believe that they were all talking to him—James—who usually stood by himself, watching them from a distance. He felt like Gordon as he told his story, and they listened to every word in open-mouthed silence—all except one of Mrs. McQueen's fat, little daughters, who kept saying, "Oh, James, you are brave! Oh, my!"

"Well, then he forced me to drink some horrible tea from a rusty, old mug," continued James, hugely enjoying himself.

"Was it poisoned?" interrupted Sebastian.

"'Course it wasn't, stupid, or he'd be dead," said Gordon scornfully.

"S'pose he would at that," replied Sebastian, crestfallen. "Go on, James," he added.

"Well, then, he suddenly began to tell me..." but James stopped short. No, he was hanged if he'd tell them all that. After all, they had gone off and left him in the lurch, sitting on top of the fence.

"He told me some very interesting things, but they're all a secret between him and me," and, in spite of all their entreaties, they could get no more out of him.

He told them about the guinea-pigs, however, but he had a strong feeling that they would not understand all the other things, about everyone feeling miserable about something.

He was quite the most popular boy in the school that day. Rory gave him some chocolate, and Violet gazed at him in the adoring way that she usually looked at Gordon; even Gordon himself clapped James on the back and said, "Well, fancy you climbing that ladder! I always thought you were such a miserable, little squit."

Poor Sebastian was so full of remorse for having caused all the trouble, that he cried himself to sleep for two nights, and his hair was standing up like television aerials all over his head.

One way and another it was the nicest day James had ever had at school. "But," he thought, hugging the secret to himself in the back row, "if they only knew about what I found yesterday, wouldn't they half think guinea-pigs a bit ordinary."

However, so many people came up to see Peter that afternoon, that James never had a chance to open the Bible.

As the days went by, things at school returned to normal, and people forgot about James, standing on his own in the playground. He did his best to re-

member what the old man had told him about looking people straight in the eye and not caring what
they thought about him, but he got on no better than
the old man had, and he soon gave up.

It was during games that he felt most awkward and
out of place, for he could never join in with the rest.
Miss Clark's brother came three afternoons a week,
and exhausted everyone with his terrific energy. He
was an artist most of the time, but he loved to come to
school to 'earn his bread', as he put it. He had hairy
legs and a loud, hearty voice, and he adored archery.
He was so enthusiastic about this sport that everyone
in the school loved it, too, and it was the most popular
game. James would sit and watch them loosing the
arrows effortlessly towards the targets, and he longed
to be good at something.

All through games afternoons he would sit in the
classroom trying to read a book, and the only thing
that kept him from hurling it across the room with
sheer frustration was the thought of what he had hidden at home under the bucket; and every day he hurried home to read a little more.

"Crumbs," he thought, as he read the story of
Abraham. "Fancy him actually talking to God and
being called His friend. It must have been wonderful
then. I bet no one dares to talk to God nowadays,
though."

CHAPTER FIVE

SABBY THE DETERMINED

Something was very wrong with Peter. It was the first day of the Easter holidays, and James was crouching beside his hutch, a worried frown between his eyes. For several days Peter had not eaten very much, and he was sitting now, huddled in the corner of his hutch, regarding James with a look of grave misery in his brown eyes.

"Poor wee mannie," said James, stroking the silky head with a worried finger. "I'll go and ask Dougal what to do; he knows everything about animals."

Dougal was mucking out Horace's shed. Now Horace was the bull, and James and his father had a very healthy respect for him, but he was Dougal's pride and joy, and they understood one another perfectly.

"Dougal," called James from the 'safe' side of Horace's gate, "there's something terribly wrong with my guinea-pig."

Dougal's brown, walnut face appeared above the huge animal's back. "Oh, deary, dear," he said in his croaking voice, "I'll need to take a look at him," and pushing the great bull out of his way—for all the world as if Horace had been a puppy—he rolled across the yard on his thin bow legs, wiping his hands on the seat of his trousers.

He surveyed Peter for a very long time, then he let out a low, hissing noise and said, "Yon wee mannie's frettin' for company; he needs a wife. I know a lonely animal when I see one, and if I were you I would go wi' your father into Newton Castle this very morn, and buy him a pretty wee wife from the pet shop.'

The Land-Rover rattled over the winding lanes. James sat up very straight with excitement on the front seat beside his father. On his knee was a box containing sawdust and a carrot, and in his pocket was all the money he had—five shillings and sevenpence —his life savings.

"I wonder how a pure white one would look," he mused. "Or maybe Peter would prefer a silky, black one. Anyway, she must be beautiful to be the wife of a champion."

He could hardly wait for the journey to end, and he wished the Land-Rover would turn into a Jaguar. He stole a sideways look at his silent father as he drove, wondering for the hundredth time how he dared to turn against anyone as powerful as God. It hadn't made him look very happy, anyway. There were lines on his face that other fathers did not have, and he always looked sad, even when he smiled.

At long last they were rattling over the granite cobbles of the ugly, little town, and, leaving the Land-Rover by the War memorial, Father went off in the direction of the Cattle Market, while James dived down a side street in search of the pet shop.

It took quite a time to find it, but after much

searching and many enquiries he arrived outside its dingy front. In the first window sat a dismal and rather moth-eaten rabbit, but the other window contained a large cage, full of guinea-pigs, crowding round a plate of food and jostling one another for better positions.

James entered the dark, little shop, where a depressed-looking man was poking about some sacks of dog biscuits. As he showed no sign of wanting to serve James, he crossed over and looked into the cage. At once all the guinea-pigs dashed away from the food bowl to form one desperate, frightened heap in a corner. That is, all except one, which continued to eat with every appearance of enjoyment, looking at James out of the corner of one beady, black eye.

There was something familiar about that guinea-pig. James stared at it with a puzzled frown.

"It reminds me of someone—but who?" It was something about the way its nose twitched and its shaggy, brown hair stood up on the top of its head, and, yes, the ears, they were enormous and stuck out on both sides of its head with a distinctly purple tinge.

"It's Sebastian!" James exclaimed under his breath. "That guinea-pig is the image of him." And it was!

"Oh, I must have that one," he thought, "but how can I? It's the ugliest one there. Peter would much prefer that silvery one or even the black and white." But his eyes kept straying back to 'Sebastian', and he knew that was the guinea-pig he wanted.

"How much are they?" he asked the depressed-looking man.

"Five shillin'," he replied, detaching himself wearily from the dog biscuits.

"I would like a female," said James, smiling in a vain attempt to cheer the man up.

"They are all females," was the even gloomier reply.

"Then I'll have that brown one," said James, pointing to 'Sebastian'.

"Oh, I wouldna' have that one if I were you. Look!" He pushed a bandaged finger in front of James' nose. "Wild that one is; wouldna' be surprised if there wasna' a rat somewhere in the family. Why not have that lovely, wee, white one?" James looked at it sitting in the corner, preening itself. It looked far too much like Violet.

"No thank you," he said firmly. "I'll have the brown one, and I'll tame her."

"You can try, but you'll no succeed, but dona' say I didna' warn you." With these words of doom he shuffled off to fetch a pair of thick gloves. "Dona' want to lose another finger," he said, as he lifted the wildly protesting guinea-pig into her box, where she scuffled and scrambled angrily round all the way home.

"Her name is Sebastina," James announced to Father as they drove along, "but I'll call her Sabby for short."

"Whatever shall I do if they fight?" he thought as

he arrived at the harness room. "They might hate each other, like Mr. and Mrs. McQueen."

His heart was beating rather fast as he opened the hutch and pushed Sabby inside. Peter made a warm, bubbling, welcome noise in his throat, but Sabby took no notice of him whatsoever and rushed straight over to the remains of his breakfast and began to eat ravenously. Everything was gone in no time, so James mixed her a bowl of bran and oats, but before he had a chance to turn round they had also disappeared.

"She's as greedy as Sebastian, too," laughed James as he dashed over to Mrs. McQueen's cottage to fetch some cauliflower leaves.

Sabby ate solidly all that evening, only stopping to stare balefully at Dougal when he came to see her.

"You'll never tame that one," was his decided comment.

"Oh, yes, I will," said James with determination, "and I'll begin tomorrow morning."

However, if James had determination, Sabby had more. As soon as he lifted her out of the hutch next morning, to groom her untidy coat, she seized the unique opportunity of exploring the harness room, and, with a quick twist of her fat body, she leapt to the floor, and she was so much like a piece of quicksilver that James spent half the morning trying to catch her again. He could not help thinking she enjoyed herself hugely, for she let herself be caught very easily when he gave up the chase to prepare her dinner.

The same thing happened in the afternoon, and by

evening James was thoroughly depressed—so was Peter, for Sabby refused to take any notice of him and ate all his share of food before he had a chance to sniff at it.

After tea James came back with some lovely, new spring grass to settle them for the night; but as he put it into the hutch something made him stop and peer inside intently. He had seen something extraordinary, but it MUST have been his imagination—surely it must. Peter was strutting up and down as proudly as if he had just won another silver cup, while Sabby sat in the darkest corner looking suddenly very mild and contented. As James watched, he distinctly saw something very small and white moving beside her.

"It can't be," he said, "but it is!"

He dived for the door of the harness room and dashed across the yard to bang furiously on the door of Dougal's cottage.

Dougal was frying bacon for his tea, and he looked up startled as James bounded breathlessly in.

"I think ... I think Sabby's had a baby," he panted. "Come and take a look."

"Oh, my, my," said Dougal very wisely, then he assumed the brisk manner of Dr. Carter, called out on an urgent case. He put on his very best Sunday hat and minced across the yard, clearing his throat and saying, "Humm, humm," just as the doctor always did. When he arrived at the 'bedside', he looked at Sabby and the white ball beside her, and said, "Humm, humm, give her some warm bread and milk, and a little raw potato, and then leave her alone until morning. They'll do very well," he added grandly, then away he strutted across the yard, still clearing his throat as he went.

James woke long before morning and lay fretting for the dawn to come, and as soon as it came he was in the harness room. At first he could see nothing, then something very small and white detached itself from the darkness of the hutch and came staggering up to James on legs that seemed much too big for it. It stared at him with interest, but before James could put his finger through the wire to stroke the little thing, another tiny creature appeared from the gloom. This one was white too, with pretty brown markings on its back; then, finally, in a series of hiccoughing jumps, came a little brown replica of Sabby, with big ears, even more purple than hers.

James had a perfect day watching them play—for baby guinea-pigs are born with their eyes open and a desire to run about and play almost at once. Peter waddled round all the time, making his bubbly noise and watching the babies with pride. He seemed to accept them as if they were his own. A wonderful change had come over Sabby, for she did not seem to be wild any more but let James sit and stroke her head, while she consumed the piles of food which he gave her.

Those Easter holidays were pure bliss for James. He scarcely left the harness room at all and was never so happy as when he was sitting on his bucket, reading the old Bible, with Peter fast asleep in his pocket, the babies exploring his sleeves and the now quite tame Sabby snoozing contentedly in his lap.

James thought he had never read such good stories as those he found in the old Bible, but the more he found out about God the more confused he became. What did God do nowadays? He surely did not go about in a pillar of fire, or divide up seas and drown great armies—if He did, everyone would be talking about it; and whatever did people do when they went to the kirk on Sundays? Did they see God? Surely they did not dare to speak to Him, but maybe He spoke to them like He spoke to Moses.

So great was his curiosity that one Sunday morning he crept round the back of the kirk and listened outside an open window, but all he could hear was the old minister's voice, quavering on and on about nothing in particular.

"I'll solve this mystery yet," said James, and he read on solidly.

CHAPTER SIX

THE EMPTY HUTCH

One day towards the end of the holidays, James was trying to read the very charred pages of a book called Judges, when he heard a loud tramping of heavy feet coming across the yard. He hid the Bible and sat down again on the bucket, half expecting to see Horace's vast bulk coming round the door; but it was Sebastian's face which appeared, smiling fatuously. James was delighted to see him, because in his shy way he was very fond of Sebastian.

"I just thought I'd come and see your guinea-pig. Oh, good gracious!" he said as he caught sight of the full cage. "However many have you got now?"

"Oh, I bought Peter a wife, and she had three babies the very next day," replied James with pride.

Sebastian flung himself down beside the hutch to take a closer look.

"I wonder if he'll recognise himself?" thought James as he squatted down beside him.

"The babies are sweet," said Sebastian with enthusiasm, "but I don't think much of the mother; she's rather ugly, isn't she?"

"She is just a bit plain," replied James, keeping his face straight with difficulty.

"She's got such terrible ears," continued Sebastian. "What's her name?"

"Sebastina."

A delighted smile spread over Sebastian's spotty face. "That's rather like my name—how funny! Have you got names for the babies yet?"

"Yes. The brown and white one is Eve, and the white one I call Sarah, and the little one like his mother is 'Tian'."

"I say," said Sebastian, even more pleased, "that's rather like my name, too. I bet you never realised you were calling them after me!" He slapped his floppy corduroy shorts, and they both laughed until they cried, for quite the opposite reasons.

"I came here to talk to you because I was so depressed," gasped Sebastian, "but I never can stay depressed for long."

"What were you depressed about?" asked James, holding his aching sides.

"My cousins from Glasgow."

"Have they died or something?"

"No, they're coming to spend the day with us tomorrow. They are terrible swanks, because their father has masses more money than mine has, and they always have something to show off about. Last time they came they brought an electric train set, and the time before that a model yacht, and they've got a full set of Meccano with an electric motor as well."

Sebastian's father worked in the forest and spent most of his wages in Newton Castle on Saturday night, so there was scarcely enough left to buy Sebastian a new pair of his elastic-sided shoes, let alone an electric train set.

"When they come I always feel so beastly miserable and stupid."

James found himself remembering the Ugly Man's words about everyone feeling miserable about something.

"If only I just had something to swank about when they come," Sebastian continued sadly. "Oh, well, I must be on my way to Micklethwaite's to get my mother's shopping—at least we always get a good tea when they come."

The next morning James did not wake up until ten. It was the last day of the holidays, so he decided to make the best of his last lie in.

"What shall I do today?" he thought, as he rolled himself into a warm ball under the sheets. "I think perhaps I'll give the hutch a good scrub out with that disinfectant Dougal promised me, and then I'll go and find some really nice grass, and they can all have a feast."

He was soon dressed and eating the cold porridge which Father had made him four hours before.

He knew something was wrong as soon as he reached the door of the harness room—there was no wild squeak of welcome. He entered the silent room, his heart beating wildly. Sure enough the hutch was empty, with the door swinging open.

"Oh, no!" breathed James, "I can't bear it."

He called desperately to Dougal, who came running across the yard on his bow legs. "Oh, deary,

deary me," he said sadly, "you must have forgotten to do up the hutch door last night."

"Then they must still be in here somewhere, because they couldn't get out," said Jamie, starting to hunt wildly among the saddles and harness.

"I'm afraid I noticed the door was open this morning," said Dougal, pulling miserably at his nose. "I'm awfully sorry, laddie, but I'm thinking you'll not be finding them now. The farm cat is trained to kill rats, and there are the dogs as well." He trailed off sadly towards Horace's pen, leaving Jamie still hunting distractedly.

"If you are any of you still alive, I'll find you."

He searched the cow-sheds, the hay barn, the woodshed and the tractor house. He crawled right under the harness room and then explored the undergrowth behind it; and all the while the farmyard cat sat in the sun, licking her lips with her rough, pink tongue.

By the afternoon, despair seized Jamie; he leant up against the empty hutch and let the hot tears splash on to its roof.

"You should be ashamed of yourself, James Brodie," he told himself savagely. "A great boy of eleven crying like a baby, and you hoping to go to the Academy in September!"

He was very ashamed of himself, but the tears would not stop coming. At tea-time he could eat none of Mrs. McQueen's lovely meat roll, and Father looked at him with deep concern.

"James, laddie," he said, "we'll go into Newton

Castle and buy some more on Saturday. How would that be?"

"No," replied Jamie mournfully, "it was Peter that I loved, and greedy, little Sabby, and Tian and the others; it'll never be the same. I think I'll just go out and have a last look."

"All right, laddie," said Father kindly. "I'll wash up tonight."

"I suppose it must have been worse for Father when all the disasters happened," thought James as he walked across the yard, "but I really can't believe that anything *could* be worse than this."

He sat down on the bucket and did not even have the heart to read Great Grandmother's Bible.

He was just about to go to bed, when the door was kicked open and there stood Sebastian, beaming all over his face, with a large box in his arms. "There you are," he said, "I've brought them back. I pretended they were mine, and my cousins were so impressed. I was sure you wouldn't mind."

Something seemed to take possession of James, who had never lost his temper before; but now red clouds of rage whirled round him, and he felt as if there was something inside him which was making him shake all over. "How dare you! How dare you! How dare you!" he hissed through clenched teeth. "How could you be so stupid? I'd like to ... break your head off."

From what seemed a vast distance, Sebastian said, "Oh, James, don't be cross. I didna' know, I didna' think ..."

"You didn't think!" screamed James. 'I'd have lent

them to you if you'd asked, but you just went and stole them!"

He made a grab at Sebastian but, as he did so, through the swirling, red fog he caught sight of Sebastian's face. His beaming smile had been wiped clean away, and in its place he wore such a look of comical dismay and remorse that everything inside James turned to laughter. He laughed until the tears rolled down his cheeks, and he had to lie on the floor and hug his knees to his chest.

Sebastian stood and looked down at him, completely confused. "Whatever are you laughing at?"

"Your face," howled James. "You've no idea how funny you look."

"Then you're not cross any more?" said Sebastian, a slow, uncertain smile creeping across his face. "You'll be my friend again?"

"Yes."

"What a relief!" sighed Sebastian, sitting down heavily on the bucket. "They weren't half a success, you know. They made my cousins' toy garage look very ordinary. They aren't allowed any pets, you see, because they live in a flat. I swanked about the guinea-pigs all day long, and at the end Sebastina bit my eldest cousin—it was lovely!" He sat staring happily into space, and James looked at him despairingly.

"Sebastian," he said, "I really ought to murder you; I can't think why I like you so much!"

Gordon was in a terrible mood that term. Everyone was rather on edge waiting for the exam results, but anxiety made Gordon even more bossy than usual, and he bullied Sebastian and teased the girls. His word was absolute law in the school, and everyone spent all their time, and most of their pocket money, trying to keep right with him.

One day in lunch hour all the top form were together in the playground, behind the cycle shed. Violet was cleaning her already spotless nails; Sebastian was staring at nothing; Rory was reading a book on pig breeding; while Gordon practised his golf swing. "The Professional at the Golf Club says I have great potential," he remarked loftily. James was not sure what potential was, but if it meant anything like conceit he heartily agreed with the Professional.

"Oh, I do wish we knew the exam results," sighed Heather; "I hate this waiting."

"I'm sure I haven't passed," said Sebastian. "I knew I never would."

"Well, I'm perfectly sure that I have," said Gordon, leaning on his golf-club. "I always come out top in school exams."

"That's only because you're Miss Clark's pet," said James.

There was a horrified silence. No one ever dared to speak to Gordon like that—Gordon, the great leader of the gang, the cleverest and most successful boy in the school.

"What did you say?" he asked in a dangerously quiet voice.

"I just said that you were Miss Clark's pet," muttered James, wishing he dared to say it boldly.

Gordon advanced slowly towards him until his tall figure towered above Jamie, an ugly, sarcastic smile on his face.

"Do you know," he said, "if you were just a little bit bigger and a little bit stronger, I would really enjoy hitting you, but I couldn't demean myself enough to as much as touch a poor, miserable, deformed, little creature like you!"

James looked away quickly. The sarcasm had hurt him far, far more than any blow could ever have done.

Fortunately, at that minute the bell went for afternoon school, but James heard nothing of the lessons which followed. He sat grinding his teeth and clenching his fists with suppressed rage.

"Someone, some time, will have to teach Gordon a lesson," he raged.

After school, Miss Clark motioned to the top class to remain behind, and, taking from her desk an official-looking envelope, she said, "I have here the list of the exam passes."

There was a sudden hush in the classroom. Heather crossed her fingers and twisted her face into an expression of agony; Violet buttoned up her little mouth; and Sebastian stuck his fingers in his ears, while a calm look of complete confidence spread all over Gordon's face.

"Heather Ferguson—you have passed."

Heather's agonised face relaxed.

"Violet, so have you."

Violet was expressionless.

"Rory, you only just managed to do it, and James Brodie, you have passed as well."

James never realised how much he had wanted to go to the Academy until that glorious moment.

"Sebastian, I'm afraid you have failed," Miss Clark continued, "and I am excessively surprised and pained to see that Gordon has not passed, either."

There was a stupefied pause; no one could take it in. Then they all turned to look at Gordon, who went bright scarlet, stood up abruptly and said, "Oh, well, I never wanted to go to the silly old Academy, anyway. I tried to fail." Then he went out of the room, slamming the door behind him.

James could hardly wait to tell his father that he had won his place. "He may be proud of me now," he thought, but Father only smiled sadly and said, "Oh well, it will help you get a job in some office when you grow up. You will be the first Brodie not to work on the land for generations," he added regretfully.

James almost wished then that he had failed the examination. How he hated the thought of that office, when everything in him longed to be free and in the open air. But how could he be a farmer, with his lame leg and weak arm?

CHAPTER SEVEN

DISCOVERED!

James got through the days at school somehow, living only for his guinea-pigs and Bible. The babies grew bigger each day and ate their way through mountains of fresh, young grass. James brushed all five animals regularly, until even Sabby began to look quite sleek and beautiful.

As the weeks went by, James read through the Bible chapter by chapter with growing interest. He loved the stories, and his imagination was quick to picture the brave soldiers and wicked kings. However, a great many pages were so badly burnt that he would often turn over leaf after leaf, only making out a word here and there, and sometimes a phrase or book title.

"Bother!" he would exclaim, "I'm missing great chunks of important stuff. I'll never find out about God at this rate."

The whole of the middle of the Bible seemed to be the most badly burnt, for the book had been flung into the fire open at the centre.

"It seems to be clearer here at the end," thought James as he was reading one morning before school. "Yes, it's really getting better all the time"—and it was. When he arrived at a book called 'The Gospel According to St. Luke', he could read every word with ease.

It was not long before he was watching the story happening before him, as he usually did.

"I'll bet this person Mary was scared when she looked up and there was a terrific great angel in her house." He grinned. "But what a funny thing to tell her that her son would reign for ever and his kingdom would never end. That means he must still be alive now."

He read on with growing perplexity and watched Mary and Joseph arrive in Bethlehem to find no room in the inn.

He had a vague feeling that they had once acted a thing called a nativity play at school, about all this, but no one had connected it with God—Miss Clark had seen to that.

"Whoever *was* this person?" James wondered as he read about the angels filling the whole sky. "He must have been jolly important."

At that minute he heard Dougal's voice rasping at him from the yard. "James, it's five to nine, and you'll be terrible late for school. Come away wi' me now, and I'll take you down in the Land-Rover."

They were soon rocketing down the bumping track at break-neck speed, for Dougal always imagined he was a world champion racing driver when he was in the Land-Rover; so people dashed madly to the sides of the road when they saw him coming, dragging their children and dogs behind them.

"Do me a favour," called Dougal, as James stepped thankfully out at the school gate; "drop in at Micklethwaite's on your way home and buy me some bacon.

I can't live without me bacon, but if I go into the shop I'll never get out again for his talking!"

With that, he drove off with a screech of tyres, narrowly missing a telegraph pole, three chickens and Sebastian, who was also late.

James walked into Micklethwaite's at five past four, and he realised at once that something was very wrong. Mr. Micklethwaite was sitting behind the counter, a look of complete misery on his chubby face and not eating anything at all—not even a toffee!

"Whatever is the matter?" James asked in consternation.

"I'm on a diet," was the pathetic reply. "Dr. Carter says I must lose five stone, because of my blood pressure; so I'm not allowed to eat anything nice—only terrible things like grapefruit and lettuce and black coffee. Ugh!" he shuddered. "It'll ruin my trade; I *have* to try everything I stock in the shop to see if it's nice enough to sell."

He took a bar of chocolate from the shelf, pushed it across the counter to James and said, "Yesterday I would have eaten that, so you might as well have it. You'll never believe that I was once as thin and small as you are."

James could not believe it, but he made polite noises and asked him for Dougal's bacon, and as Mr. Micklethwaite moodily turned the handle of the bacon cutter he suddenly asked him, "Who was Jesus?"

Mr. Micklethwaite was so astonished by the question that he swung round quickly and sent a box of half a dozen eggs crashing to the ground, where they made a lovely mess of yolks and egg-shell all over the floor. Nothing daunted, the old man snatched up a basin and scooped the whole lot into it, and, beaming all over his face, he said, "Thank goodness for that! Now I can have scrambled eggs for my supper. They're not on my diet sheet, but I really canna' waste them, can I? And I do love scrambled eggs."

He seemed so much happier now that James tried again. "Please do tell me—who was Jesus?"

Mr. Micklethwaite leaned across the counter, scratching thoughtfully at his chin. "Now I'm a very simple man," he said, "but I've always taken it that Jesus was God's Son, who came down to live like an ordinary man so as to show us what God was like; but then, as I say, I'm a very simple man. You'll need to ask the new minister that, when he comes."

"Is there to be a new one, then?" asked James, not very interested.

"Aye, the old minister is retiring at the end of the month, and there's a new one coming." Mr. Micklethwaite looked really happy by this time. Anyone new coming to the district gave him something to gossip about for weeks. So James left him happily muttering about new ministers and scrambled eggs, and walked home deep in thought.

So Jesus was God's Son. A feeling of terrific excitement took hold of James. Jesus had come to show people what God was like, and that was exactly what James was longing to know.

During the days that followed, something quite

extraordinary happened to James in the harness room. As he read about Jesus he felt that he was not just reading a story, but that he was getting to know a person, and he sometimes had a weird feeling that Jesus Christ was in the harness room with him. He did not feel afraid—just tremendously happy, and the happiness stayed with him all the time.

"I can understand Father having nothing to do with God if he thought He was all frightening and thundering and powerful, but I can't see how he could hate Him if he knew He was like this person. He really cared about people—just for themselves. How I wish I'd been one of those Jameses who were His disciples. Just fancy being near Him and watching Him do all those terrific things."

James looked up quickly, convinced once again that he was not alone in the harness room. "If God really is like Jesus," he thought, "then maybe I could draw near to Him like Great Grandmother said. If I *only* knew how!"

He read on avidly, wondering what would happen at the end of the story. He felt somehow that it should finish with Jesus rocketing about in the sky, while everyone on earth stood and watched and cheered, like everyone had when the Queen drove through Newton Castle. However, he was in for a nasty surprise.

"How could they?" he gasped in horror, as he read what the cruel soldiers did to the Son of God, and the perspiration stood out on his forehead as his imagination showed him Jesus being nailed to a cross. James had never really felt close to anyone in his life before, so now he felt as if he was watching the death of the person he loved best in all the world.

"I'll bet God was so angry that He killed everyone, like He did with the flood," he whispered savagely. "He surely couldn't forgive people for doing that to His own Son."

He read on, desperate to see what would happen next, and he was so absorbed in the story that he failed to hear the steps crossing the yard or the door of the harness room open. So it was not until he heard someone exclaim "Well!" that he realised the worst had happened—he had been discovered.

It was Gordon who stood on the threshold, staring across the room at James sitting on the bucket reading his old Bible. Underneath his careless attitude Gordon had been miserable for months. All his life he had been told that he was the cleverest, and most important person in his little world. His parents had planned everything. First he would go to the Academy, then on to university and finally he would show his genius to the whole world. But everything had gone wrong when he failed to get to the Academy. Now here was poor, deformed, shy, useless, little James going next term, while he was left behind. He suddenly hated James so intensely that he wanted to hurt him, and hurt him a lot. So he used his favourite weapon—sarcasm.

"Reading your Bible," he drawled scornfully, with his lips curled into an exaggerated sneer. "You horrible, little cissy!"

The words hurt James as no other words had ever hurt him. His greatest fear in life had been realised; he had been called a cissy. He did not really mind being laughed at for being a cripple, because he could not help that, but he did mind being called a cissy for all his life he had determined never to be one.

"Didn't you know," continued the terrible, sarcastic voice, "only cissies, old ladies and little cripples like you read the Bible now? My father says all that Christianity rubbish went out with the last century; only a few stupid people still take any notice of it."

"But what about ministers and things?" said James, clutching at a straw.

"Oh, someone has to keep the old ladies and the cissies happy, and they make a lot of money out of it. My father says no one who is anyone in the world bothers to read the Bible now."

If anyone else had been telling him all this, James would not have believed him, but because it was Gordon he believed every word. Gordon might not be clever enough to get to the Academy, but he 'knew things'—everyone at school knew that—it came of living at the Golf Hotel and meeting all those titled people. He was a man of the world, all right, so it must be true.

"You wait until I tell the others at school. How they'll all laugh—sitting there reading your Bible.' Gordon was really enjoying himself. He had never before been able to break through Jamie's wall of reserve, but now he could watch him suffer as he had watched the mouse which he had tortured to death the day before.

"Yes," he scoffed, "how they'll laugh. We'll all call you 'Little Godly Cissy Boy', from now on."

"No! Don't do that!" said Jamie desperately. "I wasn't really reading it; I just happened to find it in the wood-shed, and I looked at it to find out what it was all about, that's all."

"Well then, I should chuck it away in the burn or somewhere. Here, give it to me; I'll do it for you."

James handed him the Bible, feeling that he was giving away the only thing of value that he possessed. Gordon took it carelessly and went towards the door, saying with a final sneer, "Little Godly Cissy Boy. Bagh! I always did say you were a miserable, little squit," and he went out, banging the door behind him.

James stood where he was for a full five minutes, staring blankly at the wall. The harness room felt suddenly completely lonely and empty, and James knew all his happiness and security had gone out through the door.

"What a fool I've been all this time," he muttered brokenly. "I should have realised that modern people wouldn't take any notice of someone who was killed by the Romans. Gordon was quite right; I am nothing but a cissy squit. Fancy imagining Jesus Christ was in the room with me. I'll never be so silly again." But he went into the rainy afternoon feeling now that Jesus Christ was gone; he had lost the only friend he had ever had.

CHAPTER EIGHT

THE EMPEROR AND THE BOMB

James often wondered how he lived through the next miserable weeks. Everyone at school turned against him—Gordon spitefully saw to that. They all rather enjoyed chanting "Little Godly Cissy Boy" after him, and no one feels at his best at the end of a hot summer term, so it was good to have someone to be mean to, when they felt like being mean. No one quite knew why they were doing it to James, but they all followed Gordon as blindly as usual. Rory refused to sit next to James, Violet and Heather just stared at him scornfully when he spoke to them, and even Sebastian turned his back.

James could have borne school if home had not been so lonely. The guinea-pigs did not really care about him, so long as he fed them and kept the hutch clean; Father and Dougal were very busy with the farm; Mr. Micklethwaite was crabby with his dieting, and James could no longer feel Jesus Christ in the harness room.

One evening at tea, Father did ask rather absentmindedly what was the matter, but James muttered something about the heat, which satisfied Father, who was far too sunk in his own misery to care much about Jamie's.

The holidays began in early July, so James was marooned at the farm, unable to face going out in case he met anyone from school and had to encounter their stony stares. He knew he was being a coward, but somehow he just never had been able to stand up for himself. He could not sleep at night, and during the hottest days that Scotland had known for twenty years he had no energy to do more than feel lonely and bored.

"When I grow up, I'll run away and be wicked like Uncle Harry, and then everyone will call me 'James the Black Sheep'," he told himself one afternoon, and he was so very pleased with the idea that he went into the parlour, which was all shut up and covered with dust sheets, and found Uncle Harry's photograph in the family album. Great Grandmother stood in the centre of the picture, with Jamie's grandfather on one side of her, and her other son Harry on the other.

"What a funny-looking bloke!" thought James. "If you have to look that peculiar to be a black sheep, I don't think I'll be one."

As he stared at the face, he could not help feeling that he had seen it somewhere before. Taking the photograph out of its holder, he went into the kitchen to get a better light, and when he had studied it carefully he felt even more sure that he knew that face. On the back of the picture something had been written, and Jamie recognised the handwriting as that of his great grandmother.

'God, please bless my son Harry, wherever he is,' she had written.

"Bagh!" exclaimed Jamie, throwing the photograph down on the table contemptuously. "Lot of good all her praying ever did her. I bet God never even heard her."

One day when Dougal came back from the village, he caught sight of Jamie's wan face and said, "Good gracious, laddie, if you were an animal I'd give you a dose of my granny's salts, I would that. Here's something that'll interest you, though. I've just been down to do my shopping. It seems the whole village is gossiping, and Micklethwaite is revelling in it. The new minister has arrived, and he's got a son of twelve. They say he's seven foot tall—the minister, I mean— and he's got thousands of books and a car that's so old it shouldna' be allowed on the road. An' they do say" —here Dougal's voice dropped to a whisper—"they do say his wife is not really his wife at all, but his sister, who's a widow and keeps house for him, and it's her son, not his, and"—he dropped his voice even more furtively—"he goes to one of they boarding-schools, called prep-u-tory school or some such name." And Dougal went off to feed Horace, looking rather as if he thought the minister's nephew was at Borstal.

James was not one bit interested in any minister who made his living out of the stupidity of 'old ladies and cissies', but he wondered what his nephew would be like, so he said casually at tea that evening, "I hear there's a new minister now, and he has a nephew about my age. I suppose he would be one of these Godly Cissy Types."

"Oh, aye," replied Father, whose mind was on the

harvest; "if he lives at the manse he'll likely be one of those ... what do you call them? Cissies. Pass the 'tato scones, laddie; I'm as hungry as a horse this evening."

James forgot the minister and his family until one very hot day when he and Dougal had gone into Newton Castle with the Land-Rover and trailer to collect a new calf from the train.

They arrived far too early because of Dougal's reckless driving, so James sat down on a luggage trolley to wait, while Dougal puffed lazily at his pipe. The station seemed quite deserted; the porter was asleep in the sun, while the ticket clerk read his newspaper. Nothing could be heard except the droning of the Station Master's bees and the ticking of the waiting-room clock.

Suddenly, everything happened at once. Into the station yard roared an ancient car, honking and back-firing, with its brakes screaming; the train appeared round the corner; the porter shot up; and on to the platform ran a giant of a man with pure white hair, followed by the most beautiful woman James had ever seen. The train screeched to a halt, and out on to the platform fell a sunburnt boy with a mop of untidy hair and a wide, grinning face, who hugged the beautiful woman and the big man, and all at once the station seemed full of the three of them, talking, laughing and shouting to one another as they pulled the boy's vast amount of luggage off the train.

James watched, fascinated, as out came a cricket bat, a tuck-box, two trunks, a guitar, a tennis racket, three lemonade bottles and a bow with a quiver full of arrows.

"Oh, darling," said the beautiful woman, "it'll never all fit into the car. Surely that's everything now?"

"Think so," replied the boy in a cheerful, husky voice. "Oh, horrors! No, wait; I've forgotten my bicycle."

They all three dashed down the platform to the guard's van, only to find Dougal, the porter, the guard and the Station Master all crowded together in the door, trying to get the calf off the train. James suddenly became rigid with attention, for at that minute on to the station sidled the Ugly Man of the Forest.

"Hurry along, PLEASE!" shouted the guard when the calf was safely on the platform. "We're ten minutes late already, and where are you going?" he added rudely as the Ugly Man was about to follow the boy on to the train. The old man muttered something and disappeared into the darkness of the guard's van, while the guard sucked his whistle impatiently. At length he appeared again, clutching one of his wooden travelling boxes, while the boy handed his bicycle off the train to his uncle.

At that minute a terrible thing happened. As the old man stepped off the train, he stumbled and fell, the door of the hutch broke open and out rocketed a large guinea-pig. The bad-tempered guard did not wait to see what would happen next, but blew his whistle shrilly and caused the terrified animal to dash

up the platform towards the engine, with everyone—
except the guard—in hot pursuit.

"It's The Emperor!" screamed James trying to
make a grab at him, but the champion swerved suddenly and fell over the edge, crashing on to the lines
just in front of the slowly moving train.

"Oh, *no*! Not my Emperor!" cried the old man,
covering his face, "not my Emperor."

James made a dash for the edge of the platform, but
Dougal held him firmly by the collar, and they were
both in time to see the boy leap past them and down
on to the lines like a streak of lightning. The engine
driver jammed on his brakes, but he was going too
fast by then to stop quickly. People shouted and a
woman screamed. The train was almost on the boy,
when he flung himself full length at The Emperor
and rolled with him to safety on the down line, while
the train came to a shuddering halt over the spot
where he had been not two seconds before.

At once everything was confusion. The engine
driver shook his fist, the Station Master was shouting
about prosecuting trespassers, while the guard still
muttered about the time. The beautiful woman
sobbed into a handkerchief, and the calf bellowed
dismally in the background.

"Mark, why do you do these mad things?" demanded the minister as the boy scrambled back on to
the platform, still clutching The Emperor.

"Frightfully sorry, just didn't think," he said, smiling engagingly at all the angry faces that glared at
him. No one had ever been able to resist that smile, so

suddenly no one felt cross any more, and they were all
soon talking and laughing at once.

The Station Master said, "Plucky lad, that!" The
porter mopped his forehead and shook hands with the
engine driver, while even the guard relented and said
he had a lad at home like that, and just as reckless.
Unnoticed among all the confusion, the Ugly Man
took The Emperor and without a word of thanks,
quietly disappeared.

"He's quite vanished," said Mark in wonder, "just
as if he was magic."

"He's very shy," explained James, his fondness for
the old man lending him courage to speak. "He hates
to be stared at, you know. I say," he added suddenly,
"good job you did that, though, because that was The
Emperor."

"You mean that old man is an emperor?" said
Mark, opening his blue eyes very wide.

"No, the guinea-pig. He's terribly famous, and he's
won masses of cups. I own one of his grandsons, and
he's won a cup, too."

"I say!" said Mark, most impressed. "I'd love to see
him."

"Come up some time," invited James, quite forgetting that he was usually shy of strangers.

"I'll come this very tomorrow. Where abouts do
you ...?" but he was interrupted by a loud honking
and roaring of engines. "They're waiting for me;
must fly," and he was soon climbing into the old open
car, which was now quite piled high with luggage,
and soon all three of them had disappeared down the

street in a cloud of dust and petrol fumes.

"Phew!" said James, "I feel as if a bomb just hit me," but then everybody always did feel like that when they first met Mark Tavener.

CHAPTER NINE

A SHOCK FOR GORDON

It was the following afternoon, and James still could not forget the boy with the laughing face and turned-up nose.

"There's something special about him," thought James as he groomed Sabby's coat. "He's, sort of, more alive than other people. I don't suppose he'll really bother to come up and see Peter. He won't know where I live, for one thing, and when he meets the others they'll tell him about my being a cissy, so he won't want to see me after that."

It was just at that minute that he heard Dougal's raucous voice from the yard, saying, "He's in the harness room, lad; just step inside," and the door opened and Mark stood in the doorway. He wore an ancient green shirt and shorts, over his shoulder was a quiver full of arrows, and he wore a shooting glove on one hand and in the other he held a large, serviceable fibre-glass bow.

"I've been trying all day to find out where you lived," he grinned. "At last a big, fat man in a shop in the village told me. You lucky beast, living on a farm!" He beamed round the room, quite carefree and completely un-shy.

When he caught sight of the guinea-pigs, he flopped down by the hutch to inspect them.

"My!" he exclaimed when he saw Peter, "that one is like his grandfather, but he looks nicer somehow and not so stuck-up. You must have fun with all this lot."

They were soon talking about the guinea-pigs, the Ugly Man of the Forest, Mr. Micklethwaite and school, just as if they had known each other for years. James had never talked to anyone like this before, and he was hugely enjoying himself.

"I say," Mark exclaimed suddenly, "do you like my new bow? I got it for my birthday. It's the latest kind. Do you do much archery at school?"

"Yes, we do," answered James, suddenly feeling miserable, "but I can't, as you can see."

Mark looked at him, puzzled. "Why not?" he said. "Your right hand seems strong enough. How much can you do with the left?"

"Well, I'm just a bit clumsy with it. I can grip all right, though. It's my leg which is worst." A feeling of excitement was starting somewhere down in Jamie's tummy.

"Well, if you can grip things, you may be all right. All you need is enough strength to hold the bow and thrust it out towards the target—everything else is done with the right hand. You never know, you may be brilliant. Come out and have a shot at something."

He led the way enthusiastically into the yard, and he was so full of confidence that Jamie was catching it, too. Mark handed him the bow and quickly showed him how to hold it and fit the arrow into the nocking point on the string.

"Now, stand sideways, and turn your head to the left. That's it," he encouraged. "Now have a shot at that gate-post."

There was a twang, a whiz and a satisfying thub! and to James' surprise he saw the arrow sticking firmly in its target.

"Here, try another," said Mark; "that was beginner's luck."

However, when the next one joined the first, he said, "Oi, oi, oi, you've been having me on. You've done this before; you can't fool me."

"No, really," laughed Jamie, "I promise you I've never held a bow before in my life."

He loosed another arrow, and once again it became neatly embedded in the gate-post. Mark was staring at him in wonder, by this time.

"D'you know!" he exclaimed, "you're a natural. You even look like an archer already, you've got such terrific style. Tell you what! I'll coach you these hols, and if you practise a lot I don't see any reason why you shouldn't be really good. Everyone will get such a shock when you go back to school."

"I'm going to a new school next term," said James breathlessly, "but they're terribly keen on archery there."

"Well, there you are! If you roll up at a new school, really good at something like archery, you're 'in' right from the beginning."

"Do you really think I could do it?" asked James.

"Certain of it," replied Mark definitely. "I've never seen a beginner with such style. You must have watched them a lot at school. Now!" he continued with enthusiasm, "we've got to see about getting you some equipment. That bow is far too heavy to start on. You'd better have my old lighter one, and I can lend you a glove and a bracer as well. Come on; let's go down to my house and have a few shots at a proper target; I've got one there."

They set off through the forest, talking and laughing excitedly.

"You'll have to go in for the Boys' and Girls' Championship at the Newton Castle Carnival next month," said James. "People come from all over the district to compete in that."

"Really," said Mark, then he stopped short in the path. "Here," he said, "why don't you go in for it, too? If you really worked at it and practised hard, I don't see why you shouldn't. Don't tell a soul; just give them all a surprise."

James walked on in a whirl of happiness and confidence; but as they turned the corner by the forest sawmill suddenly all Jamie's happiness faded, and a cold feeling of horror struck him. There, coming towards them, was Gordon, followed by Rory, Sebastian, the twins and two of Mrs. McQueen's children.

So now it would all be over for ever, he thought dully as they drew nearer. Any minute now Gordon would call, 'Hullo, Cissy, been reading your Bible again?—hope you said your prayers', and everyone else would laugh, and Mark would know all about him and that would be the end, for Mark most certainly was not a cissy, and he would not want to know anyone who was.

In the end, the crisis was averted by Mark himself. He strolled up to them, waving his bow and smiling in his usual cheerful way.

"Hullo," he said, looking at Violet and Heather, "you must be the twins I saw this morning. I've always wanted to know some twins."

Heather beamed back at him. "And you must be the new minister's nephew," she said. "We're all going to the Bottomless Loch. Come too; we've plenty of tea."

"Shall we?" said Mark to James. "We can go back to my place afterwards." James nodded miserably.

As they walked along between the rows of straight, dark trees an extraordinary thing happened to everyone. Instead of feeling tongue-tied and shy, as they usually did with strangers, Mark seemed to put them all at their ease, for he had the power to make everyone he was with feel happy and rather excited, for they never knew what he would say or do next. He had a way of listening to people intently and making them feel that they were the most important people in the world.

At once he was the centre of the group, and everyone was talking and laughing and telling him funny stories.

All except one person. Gordon walked a little behind everyone else, with his arms folded and his mouth shut tight. For the first time in his life, no one was taking any notice of him. They were all looking at someone else and laughing at someone else's jokes, and he, the leader of the gang, might just as well be at home for all they cared. He walked on with the scowl deepening on his face.

As they neared the Loch Mark said, "I say, weird feeling this forest has; it's like being surrounded by armies of telegraph poles."

"Yes," giggled Heather, "there's all kinds of stories about it, too. Let's see, there's the Ugly Man, for a start."

"I met him yesterday," Mark replied.

"Then, of course, there's the Monster," said Sebastian with excitement. "He lives in the Loch, and he's very dangerous, but if you chuck him some food he won't hurt you."

"Whoever told you that?" laughed Mark. "Surely you don't believe it."

" 'Course I believe it—Gordon told me," said Sebastian simply.

"Well," continued Mark, "I don't know who Gordon is, but he must be a bit of a fool."

"As a matter of fact, he's not," drawled Gordon, thinking that it was about time to assert himself and feeling glad that he was wearing his best suit that day. He'd show this upstart. "I'm the leader here, and what I say goes."

"Good for you," Mark replied, good-natured as ever. "Say what you like."

Gordon felt rather silly suddenly, but he could not quite think why, so he sat down on a tree-stump and tried to look dignified.

"Come on; let's paddle before we have tea," said Heather eagerly.

"It's terribly deep at the edge here; we'll need to go round to the other side," said Rory. "We'll leave our stuff here."

Soon everyone was talking and laughing excitedly while they dropped their picnics in a pile and stripped off their jumpers.

"Surely our little James isn't going to dare to paddle?" Gordon's voice was so heavy with sarcasm that it cut across the excited chatter and reduced everyone to silence.

"Whatever do you mean?" asked Mark.

"You don't know James very well yet, do you? *We* do, you see. He's such a little cissy; he probably won't want to get his feet wet. He's a shocking little coward, you know."

Mark's cheerful face was transformed completely, and two spots of red rage appeared on his freckled cheeks.

"How dare you say a vile thing like that?" he snarled. "James happens to be a friend of mine."

"Well! He doesn't happen to be a friend of mine, and you can't stop me saying what I like."

"Oh, can't I?" said Mark evenly. He was really angry now. "You just say one more nasty thing, and I'll pick you up and throw you into the lake—fancy clothes and all."

"You can't do that," drawled Gordon; "I'm bigger than you, and besides all the others would stop you. So you see, you wouldn't dare, and I'll prove it to you," and, looking at James, he said with a sneer, "Little Godly Cissy Boy, that's what you are. Go away; we don't want your kind here."

"Right! That does it!" said Mark with controlled rage, and he slowly and deliberately took off his quiver and put down his bow. Gordon stood watching him, with his arms folded and his feet apart. James thought he looked rather like Goliath watching the approach of David.

Mark advanced very slowly step by step, and that very slowness lulled Gordon into a false sense of security, so he was quite unprepared for the lightning rugger tackle which Mark suddenly made. Before he knew what had hit him, he was caught by the legs, and he fell back heavily to the ground. Still holding him firmly by the legs, Mark began to drag him towards the Loch; but Gordon was immensely strong, and he fought like a tiger. However, Mark was stronger, and he had a perfect hold, so that all Gordon could do was to beat furiously at the air with his arms.

"Don't just stand there. Help me, you fools," he stormed, as he saw the Loch coming nearer to him. But everyone had suffered under his tyranny too long, and to see someone standing up to him at last was pure bliss.

With a superhuman effort of strength, Mark half pulled, half pushed, half heaved him into the Loch, and with a splash and a cry of fear Gordon disappeared into the deep water.

When he came up again, he clawed frantically at

the bank, but the side of the lake was steep and slippery, and once again he was lost to view. Next time he came up he shrieked with panic, "Help me! I can't swim. I'm drowning."

"Oh, horrors—I've killed him!" breathed Mark, and without another thought he dived into the water.

Not for nothing had he got his life-saving badge at school last term. He quickly let Gordon catch hold of his wrists, then he neatly turned him over in the water and was soon swimming strongly, keeping Gordon's head well out of the water.

When they reached a part of the bank that was not so steep, they were both soon on firm ground again. Gordon wiped the water from his eyes and the slime from his new clothes. The others were all running up, but when they caught sight of the expression of hatred and rage on his face they stopped dead where they were.

"I'll never forgive you for this—manse boy," and with that he turned and disappeared into the forest.

Everyone looked at Mark to see if this extraordinary boy was as terrified as Gordon had meant him to be, but he calmly took off his shirt and squeezed out the water, and then beaming round on everyone he said, "Where's this tea, then? I'm starving!" After that, he sat down and ate like a horse, just as if throwing people into lakes and then saving their lives was a thing that he did most days of the week.

They all walked home together as far as the manse, but when they reached the gate a strange sight met their eyes. There on the drive was some of the

minister's old car, while all the detachable parts of it
were scattered about all over the lawn. The wheels
lay in one place, the bonnet cover in another, the
back seat was perched on the front doorstep and parts
of the engine were scattered everywhere. All that
could be seen of the minister himself was a pair of
colossal legs, sticking out from under the running-
board.

"Whatever is the matter with it? Has it broken
down?" asked Sebastian.

"I don't think it has yet this week, but it soon will.
No, Unc. always takes it apart on Saturdays—it's his
hobby—but he can never remember how to put it
together again, so garage men make their fortunes out
of him."

At that minute, out of the door, carrying a plate,
came the beautiful woman, nearly falling over the
back seat as she came down the steps. She banged the
side of the car affectionately and called to her brother,
"Come out, George, and have a hot cake." Then,
catching sight of the children by the gate, she waved
at them to come in, too. "Come on," she called. "I've
got masses; I'm having a baking day."

She seemed just as easy-going and cheerful as her
son, as she handed round the plate, and she certainly
did not look as if she was having a baking day, in her
neat, frilly apron, and not a hair of her head out of
place. Not at all like Mrs. McQueen, James thought,
who always got all red and hot and covered with flour,
when she was cooking.

The minister crawled out from under the car, all

covered in oil, and Mark introduced everyone to everyone else, but no one could say 'How do you do?' because their mouths were so full of hot cake.

James was munching away happily at his, and really enjoying himself, when he realised that Mark's mother was staring at him and frowning. Embarrassment spread through him like fire, and he was immediately convinced that his face must be dirty or some other terrible thing, so he tried to hide behind Rory's large body.

Suddenly she said, "Haven't I seen you somewhere before?"

"He was at the station yesterday, Mum," mumbled Mark, with his mouth still full.

"No, I've seen you before that, haven't I? Years ago. Or perhaps it's just that you remind me of someone—but who?"

Her face cleared suddenly. "Never mind," she said. "It'll come to me, probably when I'm in the bath or at church, or some time," and laughing she handed round the cakes again.

"Couldn't they all come to tea tomorrow? It's such fun having lots of people on Sunday, and we could all go to church together then," suggested Mark eagerly.

"Well, I've made enough cakes to feed an army, so perhaps they'd better come and help to eat them up," replied his mother.

The minister asked Sebastian and Rory to help him put the wheels on the car, while the girls brushed the seats, and Mark took James off to find the light-weight bow.

"Oh, my!" said Sebastian, as they all walked home together later on, "I'm not half looking forward to that tea. I shan't eat anything all day, so I'm really hungry."

"And we'll wear our new nylon stockings and the shoes with the little, high heels," said Violet.

"Oh, no," groaned Heather; "I can't bear it!"

"Yes, we will. You have to dress up to go out to tea," replied Violet primly.

Everyone was excited because going out to tea was something that did not happen to them very often. Even Rory, who loved mucking out the pigsties on Sundays, was quite resigned to the idea when he thought of the beautiful woman's cakes. Only James was worried as he walked home through the forest. Mark had talked about going to church afterwards.

"How can I go to church?" thought James. "Someone might tell Father that I went and then the fat would be in the fire all right." But curiosity came over him in the end. It would be rather wonderful to know what really went on inside the kirk, and he could not very well go to tea and then refuse to go to church, and one thing was certain—nothing was going to make him miss that tea.

"I wonder why Mark goes to church," he thought. "I suppose his uncle makes him, like the twins' parents make them. I bet he hates it, though, because he's certainly not the type who'd want to have anything to do with religion."

CHAPTER TEN

WHO WAS SYLVIA MURRAY?

It was dinner-time at Craigiburn and they were finishing their usual lunch of baked beans, when James took a deep breath and said, "Father, I'm going out to tea today."

Father did not hear him at first, he was so deep in his paper.

"What shall I do if he asks where I'm going?" thought James, who knew Father would never let him go to the manse.

"I said, I'm going out to tea," he repeated uncertainly.

"What's that?" said Father, looking vaguely round the paper. "Oh, yes, are you? Hand me another cup of tea."

James, who had never been out to tea in his life, was so excited that he wondered if the afternoon would ever pass.

"I haven't got anything decent to wear," he thought, rummaging around in his wardrobe in desperation. Both the Brodies had holes in their clothes because Mrs. McQueen hated mending. In the end he borrowed a bright orange tie with purple spots from Dougal, and set off feeling quite smart.

No one had wanted to arrive at the manse on their

own, so they had all arranged to meet outside the school and walk from there all together. When James arrived, Sebastian was already waiting for him, sitting on the wall of the playground, with his hair smoothed down with water. He looked rather like Humpty Dumpty waiting for the King's men.

Mrs. McQueen's two youngest daughters arrived next, quarrelling violently, because they had both decided to have Mark as their boy-friend.

"What stupid creatures some girls are," thought James as he watched the twins approaching in their high-heeled shoes. Violet managed hers as if she had been wearing them all her life, but Heather shuffled along on wobbling ankles. Suddenly, just as they had reached the school gate, her ankle turned completely and she landed, squealing, in a puddle. When she got up her white dress was covered in mud, and her knee came through a vast hole in her stocking, while ladders flew in all directions.

"There now!" she said. "Stupid shoes! Look, the heel's broken off this one already."

"Oh, dear, whatever will you do?" said Violet, all flustered and upset. "You'll have to go home."

"Not likely!" said Heather decidedly. "What! Miss my tea for a bit of mud and a few ladders? I'll leave this shoe here in the ditch and hop along on the other—they'll never notice."

The very thought of it filled Violet's neat and tidy soul with horror, but Heather did not care, and, climbing up the wall to pick honeysuckle, she laddered the other stocking, too.

"Good! Now I'll match," she said, quite content.

"Wherever can Rory be?" said Sebastian. "I'm starving; I haven't eaten a thing all day. If he doesn't hurry, we'll be late, and I may die."

At that minute a very hot and worried looking Rory ran up.

"I've had a terrible time," he panted. "I thought I'd just muck out the pigs quickly, before I left, but I got so dirty that ma mother made me change every stitch I had on, and have a bath. She says I still smell of manure." And he did, quite horribly.

They were just starting off down the road, when Gordon cycled up on his new racing bicycle.

"Hullo," he said, "where are you lot going, all dressed up? To a wedding?"

"No, we're going to tea at the manse; haven't you been invited?" said Sebastian, tactless as ever.

"No, I have not!" replied Gordon scornfully. "I've better things to do. I expect you'll all get 'converted' and start going to kirk every Sunday, just so as to keep in with that stuck-up manse boy. Bah! Lot of old suckers, you are. I'm going to practise my archery."

With that he rode off towards Mr. Clark's untidy cottage, but secretly he wished he was going, too.

When they arrived at the manse gate, they all became shy suddenly and wished they had not come. Even Heather tried to pull her skirt down over her 'holey' stockings, as they picked their way round the pieces of the minister's car which, once again, he had been unable to fix in place. They all crowded together on the step with the back seat and wondered who would ring the bell. They were still wondering, when the door flew open and they were confronted by the vast bulk of the minister.

"Come in, come in," he said, beaming at them, and he was so tall that his voice seemed to come from ten feet above their heads.

They all filed in, wondering what to do with their hands and feet, but they soon felt at ease when they caught sight of Mark grinning at them from the dining-room door.

"Mum says come straight in, you must be hungry," he said.

"We certainly are," replied Sebastian, surging eagerly forward and treading firmly on Heather's bare foot. But they all stopped short when they caught sight of the table. James gazed in wonder. He had never imagined that food like this existed. There was a chocolate cake, a coffee cake and a lemon cake; a huge plate of meringues bulging with cream; three different kinds of home-made bread, and sandwiches cut into different shapes and laid out to form patterns of brown and white bread. There were some gingerbread men, a large plate of chocolate biscuits, some scones with strawberry jam and in the middle a huge trifle covered with red cherries and cream.

"Oh, my!" said Sebastian reverently, "Oh, *my*!"

They all sat down round the table, and James was just deciding what to start on when the minister said, "Let's say grace now; then we can begin."

Now grace to James was a gabbled thing that everyone said at school, rather like tables, so he did not bother to close his eyes; he just looked rather idly at the minister, so he saw a very strange thing. The great, white-haired man shut his eyes and, looking up, he smiled at someone and said—just as if he was speaking to someone he knew very well—"Dear God, thank you for this lovely food and for the fun that we are having together. Bless us as we go later into Your house, and draw near to us we pray. Amen."

James sat and stared at him, all his desire for food gone. Everyone else began to eat and talk and pass plates and cups round the table, but James was not aware that they even existed, he was so shaken by what he had seen and heard. The man had talked to God. Actually talked to Him. James had no idea that anyone ever dared to do that nowadays.

"And what's more, he even looked as if he enjoyed it," but then, with a pang of misery, James remembered what Gordon had said. "I suppose it's just his job," he thought sadly. "How Mark must despise him."

His mind was jerked back to the present by Heather kicking him under the table. "Come on, James," she said; "there'll be nothing left by the time you wake up," and he suddenly found that his appetite had returned completely, and he set to work with great gusto.

However, for every one thing that he ate, Sebastian ate six, and in the end James just sat back and watched him in fascination as he packed away four slices of coffee cake, six meringues, ten sandwiches, all the gingerbread men, nineteen chocolate biscuits and three helpings of trifle, not to mention everything he had had before James began to watch him.

"Well," he said at last, his face bright red and his mouth covered with cream, "I feel better now."

After tea they all went and sat on the lawn in deck-chairs, and when they were comfortable Mark said, "Unc., tell them how your hair went white."

"Well," began the minister, crossing one vast leg over the other, "I've always loved cars, and when I was still at school I borrowed the headmaster's Sun-beam one day, and went for a spin. I got up a terrific speed, and it wasn't till I was flying down a very steep hill at about eighty that I realised the brakes didn't work. I crashed through a hedge and over a ditch into a field of corn, and the car caught fire after it had turned over a few times and set the whole field ablaze. I wasn't hurt (not until I arrived at the headmaster's study, anyway), but when I got up next morning my hair was quite white, and it has been ever since."

Everyone was vastly impressed by this, and Rory told them how he had once been chased by the bull. "My hair didna' turn white, but I had hiccoughs for three days afterwards." Everyone roared with laughter.

"Let's sing now we've got our breath back," suggested the minister. "Mark, you fetch your guitar."

They sang what the minister called 'choruses'. No one knew the words, but they soon learnt them and sang at the tops of their voices, while Mark banged out a good rhythm on the guitar. Some of the words were about God, but James did not pay much atten-

tion to them; he was too fascinated watching Sebastian. He was sitting on the edge of his deck-chair,
gripping the arms like grim death; on his face was an
expression of acute worry, while even his ears looked
white.

"Give us a solo, Mark," said the beautiful woman,
who looked like a queen enthroned on the garden
seat.

"Right you are; I learnt this one last term," and he
began to sing.

It was not that his voice was all that good, or that
his guitar-playing was brilliant, but there was something about the expression on his face as he sang that
made James forget about Sebastian and everyone else,
and stare at Mark, as he had stared at his uncle before
tea.

> "Jesus is real to me,
> Yes, Jesus is real to me;
> I never will doubt Him,
> Or journey without Him,
> For He is so real to me."

There was a pause when he had finished, that no
one liked to break, because they felt that he had
meant every word of that chorus and that it was very
important to him.

"Surely," thought James, "he couldn't really mean
that Jesus is real to him, like He used to be real to me
in the harness room. Mark, of all people, would think
that kind of thing was silly."

He was completely startled out of his brown study

by the beautiful woman suddenly saying, "OH!" and jumping up from the garden seat.

"What is the matter, dear?" asked the minister in alarm. "Have you been stung by a wasp?"

"No, I've just remembered who James reminds me of. (Sorry about the grammar, but I'm so excited.) It's Sylvia."

"Whoever is Sylvia?" asked the minister blankly.

"You know, Sylvia Murray. I came up and stayed on her uncle's farm that summer you had scarlet fever." She beamed at James and continued, "Sylvia was the nicest, sweetest and most gorgeous person I ever met. We were only about nine then, and I've never seen her since. But you're the image of her; I suppose you couldn't be a relation?"

"I don't think I've ever heard the name before," said James shyly, "but yet," he added uncertainly, "it does seem to ring a bell somehow." He racked his brains, but the only thing he could think of was his hair-brush!

"Never mind," said Mrs. Tavener gaily; "I really think it's time we left for kirk. Let's all go and get ready."

The twins put on a couple of quite hideous straw hats, covered with artificial flowers, and Rory, who still smelt terribly, let out the belt of his shorts three notches.

"I'll never sit through kirk, with all that tea cramped by me belt," he remarked as they walked down the road.

"I'm sure you'll all be hungry again after the

service," laughed the beautiful woman, "so you must pop into the manse for supper and eat up what was left over from tea—not that there's much," she added, smiling indulgently at Sebastian.

But Sebastian did not smile back. His face had developed a greenish tinge, and his hair was sticking up all over his head. "Any minute now," he gasped, "I'm going to be..." and he was. Very!

"You poor dear," said Mark's mother. "Would you like me to take you home?"

"No, thank you," said Sebastian firmly. "I feel fine now and, besides, I've just made room for my supper."

As they neared the kirk, James' heart began to beat more quickly. He noticed some of the other people who were going in nudge one another, pointing to him, and he overheard one of them say, "Look at the Brodie boy, coming to kirk. I wonder if his father knows where he is."

"I'll bet one of them will tell him in the morning," thought James nervously.

However, as he approached the church door, he soon forgot his father, so great was his excitement about what he would see inside the forbidden building.

At first he was rather disappointed by the plain, white walls and solid, wooden pews. He had expected to see a few angels, if not God Himself, but the whole place reminded him of the waiting-room at Newton Castle station. They all sat together in a long row, and soon the minister entered, wearing a thing like a black dressing-gown. Then there followed what for Jamie was an hour of complete confusion. He could not find his place in the hymn books or the Bible, and he became hopelessly lost in the Metrical Psalms. Mrs. McQueen played the organ so loudly, that it was a wonder the roof did not blow off, and all her nine children sat behind her and Mr. McQueen, who sang loudly enough to put Horace's bellowing to shame.

James was just beginning to see why Gordon had said only fools went to kirk, when the minister entered the pulpit and everything changed completely. A hush came over the congregation, and all eyes were turned upon him. His height made the pulpit look small, and his white hair stood out from his head like a halo.

"My text this evening comes from the book of James, chapter 4 and verse 8. 'Draw nigh to God, and he will draw nigh to you,'" read the minister.

James sat straight up in his hard seat. Where had he heard that before? He knew it very well. Then he realised. Of course, it was Great Grandmother's special message. So it had not been just for him, after all.

The minister's voice cut through his disappointment. "The first thing we must remember when we think of drawing near to God," it boomed, "is that He is not just a vague Idea, or something high up in heaven, but a real Person, who really longs for our company."

The minister said a great deal more, but James

never heard a word of it, for suddenly that feeling that he had had in the harness room seemed to fill the whole building, and for the first time in many weeks James felt utterly happy. He had felt happy when he had been with Mark, and he had enjoyed watching Gordon thrown into the loch, and eating tea at the manse, but all that had only been happiness on the surface; now he was experiencing again that deep thing that seemed to spread right through every part of him.

It did not last. He left it behind when he walked out of the kirk. He did not go back to the manse for supper, in case Father should miss him and ask where he had been, and as he went home alone through the darkening forest he felt as empty and desolate as he had done after Gordon walked out of the harness-room door.

"Oh, what shall I do?" he said, kicking savagely at a stone. "Half of me longs to draw near to God, and the other half says I'll be a cissy if I do. If only I knew who is right—Gordon or the minister—and I wonder if Mark really meant that about Jesus being real to him. Oh, I wish I'd never found that Bible; it's caused nothing but trouble!"

That night he could not sleep, and he lay tossing and turning, kicking and punching his pillow, but next morning as he dressed he knew what he must do.

"I'll ask Mark about it," he thought. "I'd trust him rather than Gordon any day. After all, he goes to boarding-school, and he's older than any of us. If he says it's cissy to read the Bible and know about God, then I'll never think of it again."

He was brushing vigorously at his long, shaggy hair with the old, silver hair-brush that he had always used. Suddenly he caught sight of the initials worked in silver on the back of it—S. M.—and he remembered at once who Sylvia Murray had been.

CHAPTER ELEVEN

THE MIRACULOUS TURNING OF THE WORM

"Well, I don't know, you're a wonder!" said Mark, looking at the target, which was decorated with Jamie's arrows. "You've got a marvellously good eye!"

They had spent all day together in the field behind the manse, practising until they were exhausted. James had soon discovered that, because he used his right hand so much more than normal people did, he had developed strength in the muscles of his arm and hand that most boys of his age did not possess.

Mark was very proud of his progress, and as they threw themselves down in the shade to rest he remarked, "I can't wait to see Gordon's face when he realises you are competing against him in that competition at the carnival."

"Yes," laughed James, "and Mr. Clark'll die of shock; he organises it, you see. I'll be so scared that I'll probably aim in the wrong direction and shoot him through the heart!"

"Good job," roared Mark; "he looks a mouldy type."

"I say, Mark, can I ask you something?" James was suddenly feeling very shy and embarrassed.

"Ask me anything you like, so long as it's not French or Maths," Mark replied, lying back with his hands behind his head.

"Did you mean it, when you sang that about Jesus being real to you?"

"I should rather think I did!" exclaimed Mark, sitting upright again with a jerk. "We sing that chorus a lot in the Christian Union at school."

"Then you don't think that people who know about God are cissies?" The answer was so important to James that his finger-nails were making holes in the palms of his hands.

"Now, if you think that, it's easy to see you don't go to boarding-school. Christians can't be cissies there, I can tell you!"

"Then you mean there are people of our age who are interested in knowing about God—it's not only old people and ministers?" If it had not been for the way his hands were hurting, James would have thought he was dreaming all this.

"Good gracious, no!" replied Mark with his usual emphasis. "Whatever gave you that idea? I suppose it comes of living here in the country, miles from anywhere. Where we lived before, in Glasgow, most of the people in Unc.'s church were young. You see, being a Christian is so terrific, you have something to live for and fight for, too. It's not a bit easy, though. I should think that's why it appeals to people who are young. You don't get thrown to the lions any more, but you do get laughed at, I can tell you."

"Have you always been a Christian?" asked James,

desperate to keep Mark on the subject until he knew all he wanted to know.

"No, I haven't. When I first went away to school, four years ago, I was browned off with everything because Dad had just died, and we had to live with Unc. So I decided not to have anything to do with God. There were about ten boys at school then who were Christians, and we had great fun teasing them and ragging them, and calling them all kinds of names. But one day a pilot chap came to speak in chapel. Terrific chap he was, too; flies a dirty great liner to America every day. Well, anyway, he told us how he used to laugh at the other people in his pilots' college, for being Christians, until one day he realised that they had something he hadn't got, and he wanted it so much that he became a Christian, too. Well, afterwards I talked to him, and then I went off and locked myself in the bathroom and became a Christian kneeling beside the bath. Some of the other boys still laughed at us, but I reckon they were only jealous, because lots of them have become Christians since then, and they told me so."

There was a long silence between them, while James fiddled with the cock feather of one of his arrows. He longed to tell Mark everything, about the Bible, and the way he had felt Jesus Christ, but he simply could not make himself begin.

It was Mark who spoke first in the end. "Mr. Micklethwaite told me about your father," he said in what was, for him, a strangely quiet voice. "I mean about his hating God. I suppose you feel like that, too.

I expect you despise me for being a Christian," he added, suddenly looking very shy for the very first time in his life.

"Oh, no!" said James in horror, and then the last barrier of his reserve broke, and out tumbled the whole story of the Bible. "Then one day Gordon found me reading it," he finished, "and told me that only cissies cared about the Bible, and he took it away with him when he went, so I never did know how it ended. What happened after Jesus died on that hill?"

"Oh, you missed the best bit," replied Mark, back to his old boisterous, enthusiastic self once again. "He rose up from the dead after that."

"And then did He kill everybody?" asked James.

"Oh, no, He meant to die; it was all planned beforehand. You see, He didn't just come down here to heal a few ill people and tell some stories; He came down to be punished instead of us."

James was utterly confused by this. "Whatever do you mean?" he asked.

"Well, it's jolly difficult to explain," replied Mark with knitted brows. "Only clever people like Unc. can tell it all nicely, but I think it's like this. God wanted us to draw near to Him like a friend, and then to go and live with Him when we die. But we got all separated from Him because we couldn't keep the rules. You know, the Ten Commandments, all about not stealing and lying and loving other people more than yourself. Well, no one ever could keep them all, and as soon as they broke so much as one they were separated from God, and the punishment was death. Well, God was so fond of us that He could not bear us all not to be near Him."

"Then why didn't He forgive everyone, and let them all go to live with Him?"

"Well, he couldn't really; it's a bit like a head-master has to see that school rules are kept, or nobody will respect him. So God had to find someone who had never broken one of the rules and who was willing to be punished instead of everyone else. So that's why Jesus came—to die in our place."

There was a long pause while Jamie thought this out. Then he asked, "So everyone is near to God and going to heaven, even Father and Hitler and Gordon?"

"Well, no," replied Mark, his face red with concentration. "Not everyone wants to be near God. Jesus made a way possible, but you have to accept that way as a definite act and ask God to come right inside you as well as being just near you. That's when you begin to be a Christian, because Christian only means Christ-in. Someone with Jesus Christ inside him." Mark finished, gasping for breath and quite exhausted with all his explaining.

"Do you have to do it in a bathroom like you did?" asked James.

"Oh, no," laughed Mark; "you can do it anywhere, any time."

"Then I'll do it here and now," said James, who always made up his mind quickly and definitely. "I've been longing for this for months, and I'm hanged if I'll wait a minute longer."

So, kneeling in the grass beside the target, James became a Christian, telling God that he had broken His rules and deserved to die. "But I know Jesus died instead of me," he added, "so I would very much like to accept the way He made for me to get near to You, and please could Jesus come and live inside me, thank you."

He got up, beaming all over his face. "Just fancy, actually speaking to God," he said.

"Come on," shouted Mark. "Let's go and tell Mum and Unc."

'Unc.' crawled out from under the car, shook Jamie's hand in his own enormous one and then threw the car's starting-handle up into the air in sheer happiness.

"There's nothing so lovely as when someone becomes a Christian," he boomed.

The beautiful woman said that she had felt that Jamie was seeking God, so she had prayed for him all that day, while she had been doing her cleaning.

Then they all sat down and ate hot buttered toast, even though it was not really tea-time, and James hoped the day would never finish.

"Mark, just come and help me for a minute; I want to jack the car up," said the minister, putting down his teacup and dashing out of the kitchen, still holding a piece of toast.

"Can I help you wash up, Mrs. Tavener?" asked James, who had quite stopped feeling shy. "I'm very good at it," he added with a smile.

"That's more than can be said for Mark," laughed his mother. "He breaks more china than he dries."

"I think I've remembered about Sylvia Murray," said James as they worked.

"Really," replied Mrs. Tavener, whisking round from the sink. "Do you know her?"

"Well, no, I don't actually know her, but she was my mother."

There was a startled silence, and Mrs. Tavener nearly dropped the teapot.

"How was it that you didn't know her name before?" she asked in surprise.

"Well, you see, she died when I was a baby, and Father was so sad he never talks to me about her."

The beautiful woman sat down heavily on a kitchen chair, her face quite white with sympathy.

"I'm so very sorry," she said gently. "I didn't know. When we moved to this district, I hoped I might meet her again because she was the kind of person you never forget. I didn't even know she was married. Mark never told me your surname; what is it, by the way?"

"Brodie," answered James. "I'm Robert Brodie's son."

There was another startled silence in the kitchen; then Mrs. Tavener said in a strange. tight voice, "So she married Robert in the end."

"Did you know my father as well?" said James incredulously.

"Oh, yes; Robert Brodie was our idol; we both said we'd marry him one day. He was about seventeen when we were only nine, and he was such a big, kind, gentle person. I'm so glad you have a father like that."

Then she paused, while a puzzled frown spread over her face. "How is it that you needed Mark to tell you how to become a Christian? Surely your father must have told you all about that. He was always talking about how he was a Christian and about his wonderful grandmother and her Bible. In fact, it was because of him that I asked God into my life that very summer. Why, he must be an outstanding man for God by now."

James shuffled his feet and looked very embarrassed.

"Well, you see," he began. "Father had so many disasters happen to him that he said God had turned against him, so he hates God now and he would be very angry if he knew that I had become a Christian today."

Just then Mark clattered back into the room, and there was no more time to talk. As Jamie was leaving that evening, however, the minister rushed out of the house with a beautiful Bible in his hand.

"Here, take this, lad," he said. "It's just like the one I gave Mark. Read it every day, so that you get to know God, and talk to Him as much as you like."

James walked home in a daze of happiness. The great, thundering, mighty God was going to allow him—James—to talk to Him whenever he liked, and the same God had promised to be near him and never to go away again.

He marched along the road feeling twenty feet high and grinning like a Cheshire cat. But the grin immediately vanished when he rounded a corner and realised the whole gang was standing outside Mr. Micklethwaite's shop, watching Gordon suck an ice lolly. At once he tried to stuff the new Bible up the front of his jumper, so that he could sidle past them to safety. But then an extraordinary thing happened —something went bang inside Jamie's head, and he realised in a flash that he was not the same little, shy James any more. He had God in him and near him, so he pulled out the Bible and marched up to them, swinging it like a sword.

He looked so different that at first everyone just stared at him. Then Gordon recovered himself and, taking the lolly out of his mouth, he drawled, "What you got there, baby boy?"

"It's a new Bible," replied James briskly and without any shyness.

"I thought I told you once and for all that no one bothers to read the Bible now," was Gordon's scorching comment.

"Yes," replied James, with his head held high, "you did tell me that, but you were quite wrong. It's time you got your facts up to date. You're thoroughly old-fashioned: it comes of living out here in the country," he added kindly.

Gordon's mouth opened in surprise like a goldfish, and no one else could do more than stand and stare. This was not the James they knew. Whatever had happened to him?

As no one else seemed able to speak, James continued, rather enjoying himself. "As a matter of fact, the minister gave me this Bible," he said. "It's just like Mark's."

"Does he read the Bible?" asked Heather in amazement.

"Yes, 'course he does, because he's a Christian. So am I now." And with that he turned and walked quickly away up the road, feeling as he did so, a horrible return of his usual shyness. He would have felt far better if he only could have seen the stupefied expressions which he left behind him.

"Fancy him standing up for himself like that," gasped Sebastian. "I've never known him do that before."

"But there's a funnier thing than that," said Heather, jumping from her seat on the low wall. "That's Mark, being interested in Christianity, I mean. It can't all be so soft and silly, if he's a Christian," she added, looking defiantly at Gordon.

Gordon threw away the stick of his ice lolly contemptuously and said, "Bah! They'll both out-grow it, just like I out-grew my teddy bear. But I think James might out-grow it very quickly if his father knew about him," and with an evil smile playing round his mouth, he rode off.

The next few days and weeks were a whirl of excitement, and there never seemed to be half enough time to do everything. James and Mark practised their archery until their arms ached, and each day they became more excited about the competition. They were not the only ones who were looking forward to the carnival, however, for the whole district was buzzing with preparations. It was the biggest thing in the year to most people, and everyone would have died rather than miss the fun.

Sebastian could talk of nothing but the Bagpipers Band who were coming from Edinburgh, while Rory spent hours grooming his sheep-dog, which was entered for the dog show.

One afternoon when James and Mark met the twins and Sebastian in Micklethwaite's, Violet was all agog with excitement because she and Heather had been chosen as the 'Small Attendants' of the Carnival Queen.

"We'll ride through the town on her float, at the head of the procession, and everyone will look at us and cheer," she beamed.

"Yes," added Heather glumly, "and think how lovely you look, and what a scarecrow I am. I just can't bear it, and I'm not going to."

"But you can't get out of it now!" said Violet, most alarmed.

"Don't you be too sure about that," replied Heather darkly. "I've had an idea."

"There's to be a Fancy Dress competition this year," said Sebastian through his bubbly gum. "Rory will only go in for it if he can dress up as a cow. What will you go as, Mark?"

"Oh, I hate dressing up," replied Mark, "but I wouldn't mind being Robin Hood, just for a laugh."

"My mother says I'm only fit to be a clown," grinned Sebastian. "I rather wanted to be Macbeth, but she said I'd look a fool."

"I wonder who'll be Carnival Queen this year," said James, as he and Mark walked off towards the manse. "She has to be the most beautiful woman in the district, you know. I think your mother should be," he added shyly.

"Yes, Mum is rather a stunner; pity she's too old. I'm very worried about her," he suddenly added, while the smile died out of his face.

"Why?" asked James in surprise.

"Well, I don't think she's very happy with Unc. She feels we're imposing on him. He doesn't really need a housekeeper because he's so clever at looking after himself, you know, though I don't think he minds our being with him. She's jolly worried about money, too. She told me yesterday that she can't afford my boarding-school fees any more, so I shan't be going back there next term. Goodness knows where I'll be going; but never mind," he added, while his usual broad grin reappeared. "Nothing ever worries me for long, and if I go to a day school I can have a dog."

James was feeding the guinea-pigs that evening when he chanced to overhear Dougal and his father talking in the yard.

"I don't like it," said Dougal nervously. "It's beyond my ken, and it makes me uneasy in my bed at night."

James picked up his ears, sensing some mystery, and there was something about Dougal's tone that made him nervous, too.

"I've certainly heard someone prowling about at night," Father was saying, "and I sometimes feel I'm being watched when I'm in the fields."

"Aye," said Dougal, "and some mornings I've found fresh footprints round the yard and outbuildings. It's a pity the dogs are not better at barking, but they never were much good as watch-dogs."

"I shall tell the police, if it goes on much longer," continued Father. "But don't let Jamie know; I don't want him to be frightened."

"As if I'd be afraid," thought Jamie scornfully to himself, but that night, when he woke up to hear muffled footsteps creeping round the house, he pulled the sheets up over his head and wished he had not heard that conversation!

One day, quite out of the blue, the minister announced that he was going to start a club on Friday evenings, for people between ten and fifteen.

When the minister said a thing, it was always done at once, and the following Friday everyone of the right age in the district seemed to be there, because, as Sebastian said, "You'll try anything once, if you hear there's to be hot dogs as well." But by the time they had had a game of cops and robbers followed by an archery contest, and the boys had tinkered with the minister's car, and the girls had watched a sweet-making demonstration by the beautiful woman, everyone knew they would not be trying it once but every single week!

When they were all tired out and it was beginning to get dark, everyone sat on the lawn and ate hot dogs that made Sebastian's evening, and drank home-made lemonade, while the minister told them about Jesus Christ.

No one scoffed and laughed at Christianity now. Everyone was thinking deeply about it, and soon they were all going to kirk each Sunday to hear what the minister had to say—all except Gordon, who refused to go to club or kirk. Everything had gone wrong for him that summer. First he had failed to get to the Academy; then he had discovered that he was no longer the most popular boy in the district, and now that everyone was for ever hanging round Mark and James no one bothered to take any more notice of him.

"Never mind," he said with a satisfied smile, as he watched them all playing cricket in the manse garden; "when I go to that grand boarding-school my father has promised to send me to, they'll appreciate me there all right, and I shall look so fine in that nice uniform." And he walked off happily imagining himself Head of the school and Games Captain.

"At least," he thought, as he caught sight of the targets in the field behind the manse, "I'll beat them all at the Archery Contest."

CHAPTER TWELVE

TROUBLE, AND MORE TROUBLE

There was a terrible noise coming from the harness room. James could hear it as soon as he came out of the back door. He hobbled across the yard as fast as he could, wondering whatever could be the matter. Opening the door, he rushed inside, to find Peter and Tian fighting for all they were worth. They looked as ferocious as a couple of dogs, with their hair standing up on end and their eyes flashing, while they made a frightening chattering noise in their throats.

"Dougal, Dougal, come quickly!" shouted James, opening the hutch and trying to separate the two animals.

Dougal panted in and caught hold of Tian, while James held the trembling Peter and tried to wipe the blood from his coat.

"I donna' think they're badly hurt, you ken," said Dougal after a careful examination, "but I'm awful ashamed of you, laddie; you ought to know better, coming of a farmer's family."

"What do you mean?" asked James in surprise.

"Well, this wee brown fellow's no baby now; he's full grown; and you canna' keep two bulls in a field of cows, nor two rams with the ewes, and guinea-pigs are no different."

With that he shambled off, and James quickly found a wooden box and pushed Tian inside it.

"You'll have to live there on your own, if you are so quarrelsome," he told him severely. But Tian looked so very repentant and sad, huddled on his own in the corner, that James relented. "I'll put Sarah in with you, and you can both live together. I may even put some wire-netting at the front of the box and make it really cosy for you."

However, before many hours had passed another startling event had taken place in the harness room. Sabby, by way of protest at losing her son and daughter, produced six more babies, most of whom were the image of Peter.

"Come and have a look," shouted James, as Father appeared in the yard that evening, a pitchfork in his hands and the dogs at his heels.

"Horrors!" he exclaimed, as he looked at the growing colony. "You began with one, and now you've got eleven. By the end of the year there'll be hardly enough room for cows on this farm! You'll really have to sell at least two of the older babies, you know."

James sadly stroked Tian's silky coat. "Oh, dear," he groaned, "If I take them to that horrid old pet shop, they may go to a beastly home and be really unhappy."

"Well, give them to one of your friends, then," suggested Father.

"That's a jolly good idea," answered James, "and I

know who I'll give them to. Sebastian always wanted them."

Next day when he told Sebastian what he intended to do, he was so delighted that he jumped up and down in Mr. Micklethwaite's shop, until he upset a tower of tinned peas and sent the whole lot crashing to the floor.

"They'll breed and breed, until I have hundreds and hundreds," he panted, picking up the tins. "Then when my cousins come they'll be so jealous, they'll be sick! I'll just away home now and square it all wi' me mother."

Two hours later he arrived at the farm, his face as long as a fiddle. "Mother says I canna' have them," he muttered miserably.

"But why?" asked James. "They don't smell, and they're terribly easy to feed."

Sebastian looked embarrassed and tugged at his collar.

"It's not that quite," he said. "But Mother's funny. Just because we haven't got much money, she thinks everyone looks down on us, so she willna' take anything that anyone gives us. She says everyone at Craigiburn is proud, just because the farm's been in your family for years." Sebastian's voice trailed off miserably, and he sat down dejectedly on the edge of James' bed.

"Why not buy them from me, then?" suggested James.

"That's no good, either; she knows I haven't got any money. Oh, I do so want those guinea-pigs." He sighed deeply and blew a large bubble with his chewing gum.

"I just can't get rid of them," said James to Father at tea-time that day. "Rory says animals are no good if you can't milk them or eat them or make them work. Mark's going to have a dog, and the twins are frightened they'll bite, so what am I to do?"

"I'm afraid you'll just have to take them to the pet shop, then," replied Father, moodily buttering his bannock.

"Oh, no, I couldn't bear that—just give me one more week, and I'll find them somewhere to go."

"Well, do something about them soon," said Father, pushing away his empty plate. "I've no mind to start a guinea-pig farm."

As James washed up alone in the kitchen, he felt strangely miserable. Everything had gone wrong between him and Father recently. In their shy, reserved way, they had always been everything to one another, but, since James had become a Christian, an awkwardness had come between them, which made him feel embarrassed in his father's company. He had been to church for three Sundays now, and he practically lived at the manse. It was only a question of time before Father would find out everything.

"And then I suppose he'll stop me. Or will he?" James stopped dead and put down the cup he was drying. "Or will he?" he repeated with unexpected determination.

Suddenly he caught sight of himself in the mirror that hung on the wall, and he hardly recognised his own face. Gone was the shy, timid little James that he had always known, and a new boy stared back at him, whose head was held high, and who wore a new look of calm confidence on his face.

"I belong to God," he said out loud into the silence of the kitchen, "and He's promised to be with me wherever I go, so Father won't be able to stop me, whatever he does, because God is more important to me now than anything else in life."

With that, he threw down the dish-cloth and dashed off towards the manse, for it was Friday night and he did not want to be late for the club.

There was only one more week before the carnival, and everyone was bursting with excitement, discussing their fancy dress costumes and speculating about the various sideshows. But it was the Archery Contest that everyone was looking forward to most of all.

"I expect the winner will have his picture in the paper like last year," said Heather, who was the only girl competing from the village school.

"So they will," said Sebastian, who, with Rory, was polishing the brasses on the minister's car. "I've always wanted to have my picture in the paper, but I know I'll never win."

"Well, let's face it," said Rory glumly; "none of us has a chance with Gordon competing; he's bound to win, unless one of the boys from Newton Castle can beat him." Rory was secretly so keen to beat Gordon himself, however, that he was neglecting his beloved farm, and was practising furiously.

"Poor old James," said Heather kindly. "It must be horrid for you, not being able to enter for this with the rest of us."

James just smiled a quiet smile and said, "You may all get a surprise some day, you know."

They all looked at him curiously, but he would say no more.

"Never mind," said Sebastian, spilling brass polish everywhere, "you will be able to go in for the Fancy Dress. What are you dressing up as?"

"Oh, I'm going to put brown paint all over myself and go as an African chief, with a table-cloth round me," laughed James, and as he walked away he heard Sebastian say to Rory, "What do you suppose has happened to James just recently? He's quite different, isn't he? He always used to be shy and quiet, but now he's always laughing and talking to everyone."

"It must be something to do with this Christianity business," replied Rory, polishing vigorously. "There's much more in it than meets the eye, whatever Gordon may say."

When it was time for the minister to speak that evening, everyone crowded round him eagerly. He was never boring, and he never spoke for too long, but everyone knew that every word he spoke was worth hearing.

"There is only one thing in life that really matters," he said, as the shadows lengthened across the lawn and the scent of the flowers filled the air, "and that is to find God and to know Him. If you do this, and fail in everything else, your life will be far more

successful than if you succeeded in everything else
and failed to know God."

James knelt tensely in the grass, afraid to miss one
of the minister's words. He could not help feeling
that he had failed in most of the things in his life,
but, somehow, that did not matter now that he was
close to God.

It was getting dark as James walked home through
the forest, still glowing with pleasure as he thought of
the conversation which he had overheard between
Sebastian and Rory. But he stopped abruptly as he
opened the door and entered the dark kitchen.

Father was standing in the middle of the room,
rigid with fury. "How dare you!" he said in a low,
shaking voice. "Your friend Gordon was here just
now, and he's told me a few things about you." He
brought his fist crashing down on the kitchen table, so
that every plate in the cupboard rattled.

"The one thing I have never allowed you to do is to
have anything to do with God, but what must you do
but deliberately defy me and begin going to kirk and
hanging round the minister's house. How dare you,
James Brodie! Just how dare you!"

His face was quite white with passion, and he was
shaking all over his body. James had never seen him
so angry before, and it took all his new-found courage
not to turn and run from the room.

Suddenly Father picked up a chair and hurled it
across the room. "Will God never leave me alone?"
he almost sobbed. "I've tried to shut Him out of my
house and out of my life, but He never stops haunting

me and I can get no peace. Now listen to me," he shouted, advancing upon James, "you'll promise me here and now that you'll have nothing more to do with God, the kirk or the minister, ever again. Do you hear me?"

James' heart was beating wildly, but he answered in a very quiet, steady voice, "I'm afraid I can't do that, Father. God's too important to me now, ever to give Him up."

"Right, that does it!" roared Father, making a grab at his son, but James deemed discretion the better part of valour, and he made a dash for the back door and safety. He slept that night in the harness room with the guinea-pigs, and very early next morning he set off for the manse.

As Father was cooking his breakfast that morning, he had an extraordinary experience. He was stirring the saucepan of porridge, when he heard footsteps running across the yard, the door burst open and a voice demanded, "How could you?"

He swung round and found himself confronted by the angriest woman he had ever seen. He stood still, hardly daring to move, holding the saucepan in one hand and the wooden spoon in the other, feeling rather as if he was being attacked by a whole army.

"How you've changed!" said Mark's mother in a strange, stifled voice.

"I'm sorry," said Father blankly, "but I don't think we've ever..."

"Oh, yes, we've met before; I'm the girl with the pigtails that you once taught to ride your donkey."

And seeing recognition dawning on his face, she continued angrily, "How could you do this to Sylvia's son? Have you forgotten what the Bible says about people who try to stop children coming to God? It says it would be better for a millstone to be hanged round their necks, and for them to be cast into the sea. Do you remember now? You used to know the Bible so well. I've heard about you, Robert Brodie, and, you know, I really think you enjoy being miserable."

"Anyone would be miserable if they had had the disasters I've had," put in Father, desperately trying to defend himself.

"Everybody has disasters at some time in their lives," snapped the little woman. "All yours came at once, that's all; you can't blame God for that."

"You don't know what you're talking about," said Father, still trying to justify himself. "What can a woman like you know about real suffering!"

"Quite a bit," was the brisk reply. "Four years ago, I lost my husband and two little daughters in a car crash. I didn't turn against God because of it; in fact, I couldn't have lived through that time without his help. You've let your disasters spoil your life, and you're trying to spoil your son's life, too, but I'll stop you!"

"How?" asked Father curiously, while an extraordinary expression crept across his face.

"I'm going to pray for you," said the beautiful woman, and she turned and walked out of the kitchen, leaving Father staring after her.

Ten minutes later when James slipped nervously into the kitchen, he was still standing there, holding the saucepan and the wooden spoon, with the same extraordinary expression on his face.

He never said a word to Jamie when he left for kirk on Sunday, and for days afterwards he hardly ate anything, and sometimes he never went to bed but paced up and down in the kitchen all night long. He looked all the time as if he was searching for something, while his eyes were the eyes of someone who is tormented.

CHAPTER THIRTEEN

SEBASTIAN AND THE BAGPIPES

"Oh, James, I wonder if you can help me," Miss Clark wobbled to a halt on her motor-scooter, looking very hot and harassed. It was the day before the carnival, and she was on the committee and had at least a thousand last-minute things to attend to.

"I need another prize for the side-show I'm running tomorrow—something rather unusual, you know—and I wondered if you had any of your guinea-pigs to spare."

"Well, I have, as a matter of fact," replied James, thinking of Tian and Sarah. He hated the thought of their going to someone he did not know, but he hated their going to the miserable man in the pet shop even more, and the week which Father had given him to find a home for them had lengthened into three. So he said, "I've got two. I'll bring them down to your house after tea."

Miss Clark thanked him absently and rode off again.

When James arrived at her house, carrying the guinea-pigs in their hutch, he found Miss Clark and her brother loading all kinds of properties and equipment on to the lorry, to take to Newton Castle in the morning. Mr. Clark was fussing about with the targets that would be used in the Archery Competition which he so enjoyed organising. He smiled at James and said rather patronisingly, "Coming to watch tomorrow? We're expecting such a large entry in the 'Under Fourteens' event, that we can't do the St. Nicholas this year; we'll have to limit it to twelve arrows from forty yards, and six from thirty. But I've no doubt who'll win," he added, gazing fondly at Gordon, who was helping to load the targets on to the lorry.

"Boy! I hope you can beat him, Mark," exclaimed Jamie, as they had their final practice later that evening. "I'd give anything to see you do it."

Mark looked doubtful. "He's pretty good; I've watched him shoot," he said.

That night it was almost impossible for James to sleep, he was so excited. His bow and arrows lay ready on the floor beside him, while the brown paint for his fancy dress was waiting in the wood-shed. "If only someone can beat Gordon," he whispered, as he fell asleep at last.

All night he dreamt furiously that he was shooting in the competition, but all his arrows turned into broomsticks, and shot into the sky, and would not go anywhere near the targets, and he woke up sweating and wishing that he had never thought of entering for anything.

The moonlight was pouring eerily in through the open window, and James found that his heart was beating violently. Some noise had made him wake up, and there it was again. There was someone outside, moving about in the garden.

"I'd better go to Father," he thought. "It's time we knew who this person is."

He slid out of bed and crept across the room, but on his way to the door he had to pass the window. Curiosity suddenly overcame his fear, and, hiding behind the fluttering curtains, he took a quick look out into the moonlight. Immediately he froze with horror. There, standing in the ruined waste of Great Grandmother's garden, staring intently at the house, stood the Ugly Man of the Forest.

As James watched him, suddenly all his fear left him, for there was such a look of sorrow and wistful longing on the old man's ugly face, that Jamie could not bear him to be frightened away by the dogs or the police or even Father's gun, and creeping back to bed he soon fell asleep.

By one o'clock prompt everyone was climbing into the minister's roomy car, for he had promised to give them all a lift there and back.

"You'll have to travel in the boot," he laughed, as he caught sight of James painted brown all over.

Everyone was roaring with laughter at everybody else's costumes and secretly thinking their own was best. Sebastian made a marvellous clown, and Rory certainly smelt like a cow even if he didn't look like one.

"I've hidden your bow in the boot with mine," whispered Mark, "so that everyone will faint with surprise when you enter for the competition."

"Are we all here now?" asked the minister, climbing into the high front seat.

"No, the twins are still missing," shouted back everyone at once.

"Well, we can't wait long or we'll be late. Oh, here's Violet now."

But it was not the usual prim and rather smug Violet who came trotting tearfully through the manse gate, holding up the skirts of her gorgeous attendant's gown.

"Oh, dear," she sobbed, "Heather's done a dreadful thing; as soon as we got down the lane out of mother's sight, she took out a pair of scissors and cut off all her hair."

At that minute Heather arrived, a smile of satisfaction on her face. "Now no one can make me ride in that vile float," she remarked. "Not with my hair like a scrubbing-brush." With that she stripped off her beautiful gown and revealed a striped jersey, shorts and socks, complete with football boots. "I'm going as Stanley Matthews," she announced, climbing into the car. "I always thought I looked rather like him."

When they arrived at the Newton Castle sports ground, the whole place was buzzing with activity. There were side-shows of all different kinds, stalls selling everything under the sun, and tents and marquees bulging with displays of everything that could be displayed. There were shows of everything from flowers to babies, and wherever you went you fell over people selling ice-creams, sweets and fizzy drinks. Everything was arranged round a central enclosure, where the Carnival Queen would be crowned by the Provost; and later the acrobatics and sports would take place.

Rory hurried off with his collie to the Dog Show, and the others went to watch the carnival procession which was already driving through the town.

"Thank goodness I'm not up there," said Heather, as the Queen's float passed by with Violet sitting primly among the attendants. "She means to be Queen herself one day, and she will be."

Next came a big, black car carrying the Provost and Lady Gertrude Bray, who was to open the Carnival, which was in aid of starving refugees. She was so thin that she looked like a starving refugee herself!

After that came many other floats—which were really only lorries, decorated to look like many strange things. One was a teapot, another a house, a third formed a tableau of refugees, while a terrible dragon came at the end.

The Bagpipe Band from Edinburgh brought up the rear, with drums beating and kilts swaying. It was a marvellous spectacle, and everyone surged into the road to follow the procession to the opening cere-mony, where Mrs. McQueen's eldest daughter was crowned Queen.

Soon everything was under way, and the noise was terrific. Dogs yelped, babies cried, the bagpipes wailed and over all boomed the voice through the loudspeakers.

"The Adult Archery Competition is now commencing at the Butts, behind the tea tent," it roared.

"It's not our turn yet," said Sebastian, who was not a good shot. "Let's go and have a look at the side-shows."

They all wandered off together. As they passed a stall which was selling hot pies and chips, they met Mr. Micklethwaite. It was the first time they had ever seen him outside his shop, so they hardly recognised him. But he beamed when he caught sight of them.

"Look," he said proudly, "I haven't been able to get into these trousers for twenty years; don't you think I'm looking slim?"

No one could see any difference, but they all told him he was beginning to look like a film star, which pleased him immensely.

It was not long before they reached Miss Clark's stand, and Sebastian's face lit up with sheer delight when he caught sight of the two guinea-pigs.

"Are they a prize?" he asked in wonder. "I'll win them if it kills me."

"It costs threepence," said Miss Clark firmly, but Sebastian opened his sticky hand to reveal half a crown.

"Father gave it to me this morning," he announced proudly, for it was the first pocket money that he had ever had.

"It's very difficult," continued Miss Clark, who really did not like Sebastian. "We don't expect many people to manage it, that's why the prizes are so good."

It was difficult, too. A crumpled and twisted wire was strung between two posts, and it was connected by electricity to a bell. A ring held by the competitor had to be passed carefully along the wire and, if touched, the bell rang loudly and the competitor was disqualified.

Sebastian used up one shilling and sixpence in fruitless attempts, and he was nearly in tears when the loudspeaker summoned them to the judging of the Fancy Dress Competition.

There were so many different and clever entries, that the judge, who was Lady Gertrude herself, had a difficult time coming to her decision. But Gordon's mother had stayed up all night to make him an astronaut's outfit, complete with a goldfish bowl for his head, so in the end he won, and he strutted smugly off in the direction of the Archery Butts, quite confident that he would very soon win another prize.

"Come back with me, while I have another try for those guinea-pigs," pleaded Sebastian, who was possessed by the idea of owning them.

As they followed him, James caught sight of a very imposing man with a beard, talking earnestly to the Provost, and he tugged Mark's sleeve and whispered, "Look, there's the Headmaster of the Academy."

"Oh, I forget to tell you, in all the excitement," Mark replied "Mum went to see him yesterday, and she's got me in. I'm to start there with you next term."

James felt at that minute that he could not have been happier if he had tried. "If only Father was here to watch the Archery Competition, then I really would die of bliss," he added to himself, "but of course he would be too busy with the harvest."

They had reached Miss Clark's side-show by then, and Sebastian was already crouched by the wire, his face red with concentration.

With his first go he rang the bell after only six inches, and the second was not much better. He was really harassed by then.

"I've only got two more tries," he gasped. "I just couldn't bear it if I lost them now."

He paid his threepence and tried again, but half-way along the wire the bell rang loudly.

"This is the last one," he said miserably, wiping the perspiration from his forehead, and, with his face bright red and his tongue sticking out, he knelt down for the final attempt.

There was a tense silence all round the stall; no one dared to breathe. Heather bit her lip so hard it bled, and Rory pulled off one of the horns of his cow costume. Even Tian and Sarah looked anxious, peering through the wire front of their box.

"Only one more foot to go," breathed Sebastian. "Over the squiggles and round the twisty bit, and..."

"Bo!" said Gordon suddenly from the back of the crowd. Sebastian jumped violently, and the bell rang loudly into the silence.

"Oh, you beast!" cried Sebastian. "Now I've lost them for ever."

"Sorry," grinned Gordon, quite unconcerned, but Heather came to the rescue by saying, "Oh, Miss

Clark, do let Sebastian have another go free; that wasn't fair."

Miss Clark hesitated, for Gordon was her favourite, but in the end the better half of her nature prevailed, and she said rather crossly, "Very well, Sebastian, but hurry up, do."

Once again the thick silence descended, and more and more people gathered round, sensing the importance of the occasion. Sebastian was panting, like Mr. Micklethwaite on stock-taking day, and his ears were purple with the strain.

Three inches, two inches, one inch ... "I've done it!" he screamed, and he lay flat on the ground, kicking his legs in the air, while the whole crowd clapped.

"I'll keep them here for you, Sebastian," said Miss Clark, with cold disapproval. "You can collect them later on."

"We ought to be going in the direction of the Butts now," said Rory, who had a watch. "We don't want to have a rush."

The problem was getting Sebastian to hurry. He was so highly elated by his success that he told everyone he met about it, and he would keep jumping up and down and singing raucous songs.

As they were nearing the Butts, they passed a side-show piled high with glass and china prizes, beside which was sitting a rather unwilling Dougal, who was looking after the stall while his large, terrifying cousin had her tea.

"Roll up, roll up, roll up," he grinned when he saw them approaching, and, pointing to a hideous face painted on the wall at the back of the booth, he said, "Just get one of these balls through his open mouth, and you'll win one of these wonderful prizes."

"Oh, I'd love a go at that," squeaked Sebastian, still jumping up and down, "but I've got no money left now."

"Here you are; I'll treat you," said Gordon very grandly, for he secretly felt rather ashamed of having said 'Bo!' at the wrong minute.

"Thanks a lot," said Sebastian, completely forgiving him for everything.

Now Sebastian was quite horribly poor with a ball of any kind—he always had been—but now excitement made his aim even worse than usual.

He took the heavy wooden ball from Dougal and, stepping backwards, he flung it with great force in totally the wrong direction. Narrowly missing Dougal's angry face, it crashed into the heart of the beautifully set out prizes. With a terrible noise, cups, teapots, glasses, butter dishes and hideous china vases all fell together and broke into thousands of pieces on the ground.

"You wee varmint!" shouted Dougal. "Whatever will ma cousin say?" And, seizing his walking-stick, he added, "You wait until I catch you."

But Sebastian did not wait! He took off as fast as his legs would carry him, followed by Dougal shaking his walking-stick, his terrifying cousin still holding her teacup, and everyone else not wanting to miss the fun.

Sebastian was so terrified that he never looked

where he was going, and he careered madly through the crowds who were watching the Bagpipe Band parading sedately up and down. The next minute he had crashed right into the middle of them. Bagpipes wailed to a halt, drumsticks flew in all directions and the pipers fell over one another in a confusion of kilts and waving legs.

Sebastian never stopped to see what would happen next but rushed away in the direction of the gas works, leaving the Band Leader shaking his baton and the bass drummer hopelessly tangled in his leopard skin.

After that, in spite of all the Provost's earnest pleading, the Bagpipe Band never visited Newton Castle again!

CHAPTER FOURTEEN

THE ARCHERY COMPETITION

"Fancy meeting you here," said a pleasant, rather musical voice, which made Father start violently and nearly spill the cup of tea he was carrying. "I thought Jamie said you were too busy to come."

The beautiful woman was wearing a cloudy blue dress, and she looked like a creature from another world, as alone she sipped her tea in the crowded refreshment tent.

"Oh, well," replied Father rather awkwardly, "the harvest's gone so well this year that I thought I'd take the afternoon off and see the Dog Show, and Jamie's kept on urging me to watch some archery contest or some such thing. Can't think why, though," he added, "because, of course, he'll not be going in for it."

"Oh, well, you must come and watch my son do his stuff," laughed Mrs. Tavener, but Robert Brodie did not answer her, for his eyes were fixed on her face as if he was still searching for something.

Trying to shrug off the strange mood, he said in rather a forced jolly way, "Well, I hope you've remembered to pray for me."

"I have remembered," was her quiet reply. "In fact, I've hardly stopped since I saw you last."

"Well, I wish you would stop, once and for all!"

replied Father suddenly feeling unaccountably angry. "Ever since you came to me that morning I've had no peace. It's just as if God is calling me all the time."

"Well, why don't you go back to Him again, then?" asked Mrs. Tavener gently.

"What? Creep back to God and admit to Him that I can't live without Him? Never! That would be nothing but defeat."

Then sudden anger sprang into her eyes as well. "You're the stupidest man I know, Robert Brodie," she said. "You know the way to happiness, but you're too proud to take it," and she rose and walked quickly away from the tent.

"The Under Fourteen Archery Competition is now commencing," boomed the speakers.

"Come on, quick!" yelled Mark to the others, who were still watching the angry confusion of the bag-pipers. "I'll go and get the stuff from the car and meet you all there."

Soon they were all standing in the queue of competitors, waiting to give their names to the harassed Mr. Clark who was, of course, the Field Captain. One by one they gave him their sixpenny entrance fee, and he wrote their names in his book.

When it was Jamie's turn, he looked up crossly, with his pencil poised in the air, and said, "Run away, James Brodie, I can't have you under my feet now."

"But please, I want to enter," stammered Jamie, feeling a complete fool.

Mr. Clark frowned. "This is a serious competition, you know; we can't let you stand nearer the targets or have any other advantage."

"I know," replied James, flushing. "I'll compete like everyone else," and he put his entrance fee down on the table with a snap.

Rory and Heather were behind him in the queue, and, when he had paid, Rory said, "Surely you aren't really going to try to compete?" and Jamie, wishing that he was not, told them that he was.

"Right now," said Mr. Clark to everyone in his loud, hearty voice, when he had taken all the money. "We can begin. We have twenty-one competitors, so will the first three proceed to the forty-yard shooting-line for the first end."

Rory was in the first end with two boys from another school. They each loosed three arrows in turn, and then another three. Rory scored twenty, but one of the others, a big, red-haired boy, scored twenty-five.

Heather was in the next end, and she was so nervous that she missed the target completely with two of her arrows, put three into the white and one into the black, scoring a miserable total of five.

James stood watching the following ends with his heart beating faster all the time.

"I'm going to make a fool of myself," he whispered. "I'll never hold my head up again. Fancy trying to go in for a competition like this."

His self-confidence was in no way increased by

Gordon's sarcastic smile. "This isn't a rehabilitation centre," he sneered, when he noticed James holding his bow and arrows.

"Right now, last three on the shooting-line," roared Mr. Clark, and James realised his time had come.

He was to shoot with Mark and Gordon, and he was glad of this. "Everyone will be too busy watching them shooting against one another to notice what I do," he thought. But as he took up his position behind the line, he was conscious of many surprised faces in the large crowd that surrounded the Butts. All the people who knew him were nudging one another and pointing, and, when he caught sight of his father's astonished face in the crowd, his heart missed a beat. So he had decided to come, after all. "Now I've just got to do well," he thought, "or Father will be ashamed of me, like he always is."

"Shoot, please," commanded Mr. Clark, and Gordon drew his bow and sent a perfect arrow right into the heart of the gold, for nine points. There was a gasp from the crowd, and Gordon, with a superior smile, loosed two more—one into the red for seven, and another into the blue for five.

"Twenty-one with his first three arrows—good score that," boomed the minister.

"Aye," said Father, who had just been introduced to him by the beautiful woman. "Goodness knows who persuaded my little lad to compete; he'll hardly have enough strength to reach the target."

"Never mind," said the minister kindly. "It'll do

him good to feel he's competing, even if he never scores a point."

"I had no idea they were both practising in the field all that time," put in Mrs. Tavener. "I thought Jamie was just watching Mark."

Mark scored only fifteen with his first three arrows, and then it was Jamie's turn. He was so nervous by this time that he was past caring what happened, and he loosed his first arrow with his eyes shut tightly, and he did not dare open them until he heard Mark say, "It's in the red; well done!"

The next two were both blacks for three each. There was a startled pause as Jamie finished his turn, and then everyone burst into enthusiastic clapping.

"Thirteen, what a fluke!" commented Father, trying not to look as pleased as he felt, as they all watched Gordon shoot his second three arrows which would complete his first end. He scored twelve with them, making a total of thirty-three—the best score until then.

Mark added ten to his fifteen and then stood back to watch James, who took a deep breath and sent two into the red. He was so excited that he loosed the next one too quickly, and the arrow missed the target completely and fell with a harmless thud to the ground.

"Don't forget to keep your whole body still until the arrow is in the target," muttered Mark, as they walked away, and the first three took up their positions again.

"Still, twenty-seven's jolly good; you're beating me by two."

No one beat Gordon's record of thirty-three during the second end, so by the time it came round to his turn again he was positively oozing with self-confidence.

When they had loosed their next six arrows the scores were: Gordon, sixty-three; Mark (who had had a couple of golds), sixty; and James, fifty-seven.

Father could hardly believe his ears when he heard the score. He had always felt ashamed about Jamie, as if it had been his fault that his son had been handicapped. He always secretly longed to have a boy who could do things that other boys did, and now here today was Jamie doing just that, and beating most of the others into the bargain. He had a terrible urge to prod the fat woman in front of him and say, "That fair boy is my son!" But, catching sight of Dougal and Mr. Micklethwaite coming towards him, he stifled the desire and beamed at them instead.

"Thank goodness you're here," panted Mr. Micklethwaite. "If I'd told you about Jamie doing this later on, you wouldna' ha' believed me."

"When I remember the wee, twisted baby that he was, I canna' believe it's possible," put in Dougal.

"Something's changed that lad completely recently," continued Mr. Micklethwaite. "He never would have had enough confidence in himself for this before."

Only the beautiful woman saw the strange look

which crossed Father's face when he heard that remark.

"I never knew you could shoot, James," said Mr. Clark rather sourly, as he bustled about organising the final end from thirty yards. "But whoever's been teaching you has certainly made a good job of it."

"You've just got to catch up three, Mark," whispered Heather, when only the last three were left to shoot. "You really must beat Gordon; he looks so terribly cocky."

"It all seems to be between Gordon, James and Mark now," commented Rory. "Have you ever seen anything so extraordinary as James?" he added. "Who'd have thought he could do so well?"

"Well, I wouldna' believe it, if I hadna' seen it mesel'," said Sebastian, who had crept out of his hiding place to join the others. He had been far too frightened of the bagpipers and Dougal's terrifying cousin to enter for the competition, but now he was too engrossed in watching James to be afraid of any of them.

Gordon strutted up to the line completely confident and scored a cool twenty-two with his three arrows, without appearing to try. James held his breath for Mark, but something seemed to be wrong with him. Two arrows went into the white, and one into the blue.

"Only seven points," he muttered. "Whatever is wrong with me?"

It was Jamie's turn, and, as he pushed the nock of the arrow into the nocking point on the string, he caught sight of the imposing figure of his future headmaster, watching him from the crowd. Even this did not worry him; he was perfectly calm by then. Of course, he could not win, but he had not made a fool of himself as he had feared he would.

He shot his three arrows without really caring where they went, so he could hardly believe his ears when he heard the Target Captain—who was one of the masters from the Academy—announce that he had scored twenty-five.

"I say, plucky lad, that," said the Headmaster of the Academy to Miss Clark, who was watching James with her eyes practically out on stalks. "He'll be a great asset to our school; takes a lot of courage to stand up in front of a crowd like this when you have a handicap like his."

Gordon chanced to overhear this remark and shrugged disdainfully. Let little James be an asset to the silly, old local academy. Only three more weeks among these stupid country people, then he—Gordon —would be surrounded by all the sensible and admiring people at the expensive boarding-school. But, in the meantime, he was going to win this Archery Contest and give all these locals something to talk about.

His final total was ninety-eight, and as he threw down his bow and folded his arms his smile seemed to say, 'Beat that if you can'; and, as he idly watched the others, he was already planning how he would stand when the newspaper reporter took the photographs.

"Mark needs thirty-two to beat him," thought James despairingly. "He'll never do it."

Mark tried very hard but managed only twenty-two, for a total of eighty-nine, exactly nine points behind the grinning Gordon.

"Well, at least he's come second," thought James as he took up his stance, but at that minute he heard Heather's voice hissing at him from the crowd, "Come on, James; it all depends on you."

"What all depends on me?" wondered James blankly. "Surely I'm nowhere in the running." Then he realised in a flash that he needed only seventeen to win.

CHAPTER FIFTEEN

SURPRISES FOR JAMES

The thought put him off so much, that the arrow he was preparing to loose slipped from his fingers and fell to the ground a few feet away.

"I'm sorry, but we'll have to count it," said Mr. Clark, slightly triumphant.

"He may be able to touch it with his foot still on the line," suggested Mark. "Try it, Jamie; if you can do it, you can shoot the arrow again."

James planted his foot firmly on the line and then stretched out with his bow as far as he could. Father's heart was in his mouth when he saw that he was three inches short. Holding his breath, James tried again, and this time he just touched the arrow with the nock of his bow. A cheer went up from all around him, and Father clapped the minister on the back, shook hands with Mr. Micklethwaite and very nearly did poke the fat woman.

But Jamie's concentration had left him, and the arrow missed the target altogether. Father gasped and bit his lip with disappointment. "If only he could have won," he told the beautiful woman, "I think I'd have been the proudest man in Scotland."

James saw that look of disappointment and utter misery spread through him. "Please, God, let me win, so that Father will be proud of me," he whispered.

Cool, calm determination possessed James then, and without another thought he sent his last two arrows into the gold. A tremendous cheer went up from all sides. "One hundred points!" breathed Mark, while Heather jumped up and down, squealing, "Jamie's beaten Gordon, Jamie's beaten Gordon."

Mr. Clark looked flabbergasted, the minister clapped his huge hands until they were sore, Rory stood and gaped, while Sebastian flung himself down on the ground once again and kicked his legs wildly in the air. Even Violet was smiling, and Mr. Micklethwaite was so delighted that he forgot about his diet and dashed off to buy everyone a large ice-cream, and celebrated by eating six himself.

Dougal wiped his walnut face and said, "This is a great day for Craigiburn!" and he suddenly had to dash off behind the tea tent to blow his nose loudly.

There was only one person there who was not smiling and talking excitedly. Gordon picked up his bow and arrows and stalked away, muttering under his breath.

The Headmaster of the Academy sailed majestically up to Mr. Clark and said, "My dear fellow, you seem to have trained some excellent youngsters at your little school. You've certainly done a great job with the cripple boy."

"Oh, well," replied Mr. Clark, "one likes to take extra pains with these handicapped children."

"Extra pains, my foot!" muttered James, overhearing the conversation, but he was too happy to care.

For the first time in his life he felt equal with other boys of his age, and he could stare them straight in the eyes, just as the old man had told him.

Among all the noise and excitement Father stood, perfectly still, looking at James in a dazed and incredulous way, and when his son bounded cheerfully up to him he seemed in danger of choking.

"It's a miracle," he whispered hoarsely.

"Everything's been rather like a miracle since I became a Christian," laughed James, quite forgetting to whom he was speaking.

A sudden look of pain and anguish spread over Father's face, and James realised with horror what he had just said.

"I can't stand it any longer!" said Father suddenly, and turning on his heel he rushed for the car park and was soon hurtling down the main street in the Land-Rover.

"Don't worry about him," said the beautiful woman. "I think you'll find he's gone home to put himself right with God again. Goodness knows, it's about time he did."

Just at that minute Dougal rushed up, followed by two very large policemen. "Where's your father, laddie?" he gasped to James. "Yon polices want him."

"It's a very urgent matter, lad," said the bigger of the two constables. "We were told at his farm that he was here. We want you, too," he added, taking Jamie by the arm.

"Father just left for home, but what have we done?" asked Jamie in alarm.

"I'll tell you on the way," said the policeman, pulling him towards the waiting car.

Everyone followed in amazement, staring in horror at the scene.

"Here, you can't do this," boomed the minister.

"Whatever can be happening?" demanded Mr. Micklethwaite, not wanting to miss the fun.

"Let's all fight them and rescue James," shouted Mark, waving his bow.

"It's perfectly all right," said the constable, bundling James into the car. "It's the ugly old tramp from the forest. He's had a heart attack, and Dr. Carter says he's dying. It seems the old man has something very important to tell these two Brodies, and we must get them there in time."

The police car bumped and lurched over the uneven forest track at lightning speed, and in no time it had deposited Father and Jamie in the clearing where the old man's caravan stood. Dr. Carter was at the gate in the fence, with his arms folded very disapprovingly.

"You've certainly taken long enough to get here," he said in his usual sour way. "But fortunately he seems to have rallied a bit now. He collapsed in the forest and was found by Gavin Campbell, muttering that he must speak to the two of you at once. He is sitting up now, as perky as you please, but the ambulance is on its way."

James and his father entered the dark, little caravan, to find the old man propped up in his bunk with old sacks and piles of straw. But they both stopped dead in amazement when they saw what he was holding in his wrinkled, old hands, for it was Great Grandmother's Bible.

"Come in, come in," he said. "I have some property to return to you. I'm dying, you see," he said cheerfully, "so I had a mind to see my two relations."

"Relations?" murmured Father blankly.

"Aye," said the old man, "You're my nephew. Did you never hear of Harry, the black sheep of the family, who ran off to foreign parts? I was born at Craigiburn, just the same as you were, and this is my mother's Bible. She always used to say that it should never leave Craigiburn, and while the Brodies loved it and read it they would be happy, but when they stopped reading it misery would come their way."

He looked at Father and then smiled his funny, twisted smile, saying, "Here, you'd better take it back. I've watched you often at Craigiburn, and I've always thought how miserable you looked."

Father approached the bed and reverently took up the big Bible that once he had tried to destroy, and staring at it with awe he murmured, "This is the strangest thing of all, that today I've found God again, and I've also found this Bible," and he stood quietly holding the Book, as if it was the greatest treasure in the world.

"However did you get it?" asked James breathlessly. "Was it magic or something?"

"No, no, lad," replied the old man weakly. "I was walking through the forest one day, when I met a big, sulky-looking boy who was carrying this Book, and I recognised it as my mother's Bible, so I shouted 'Drop that!' and he did and ran off like a mad thing. I've been reading it ever since, and remembering all the things she taught me so long ago, but I think she'd like it to go back to Craigiburn now."

Suddenly his old face looked ashen grey, and, putting his hand on Jamie's sleeve, he said, "Look after my cavies for me, laddie, and keep them winning those silver cups."

Dr. Carter stepped forward, clearing his throat noisily and saying, "Hmm, hmm." He did not like looking after dirty, old tramps very much, and he very much disapproved of the Brodies having one for a relation. But when the Forest Manager came in at that minute and said, "Good afternoon, sir, I'm so sorry you're ill," in a very deferential and polite fashion, Dr. Carter's eyes opened in amazement.

"Oh, there you are, Ferguson," said the old tramp, from his straw-covered bunk. "Look, I'm leaving all the forest in trust to the boy here, for when he comes of age. My will is with my solicitor. I like you, boy," he said, looking at James with his half-closed eyes. "I want you to have my forest. I made all my money in Canada, and I owned many forests out there, but I sold them to buy this one, so that I could be near to Craigiburn. Don't waste your life, boy, as I did; just remember to look 'em all straight in the eye."

CHAPTER SIXTEEN

THE GREAT CHANGES

James sat in the apple tree and looked at Craigiburn. So many things had changed, that it was difficult to realise that it was only just over two years since he had sat there before.

He had thought the house looked cursed then, but now it looked nothing but peaceful and happy. The windows were all open and newly painted, while fresh, gay-coloured curtains hung in them. Pink roses climbed over the walls, covering and softening their grey harshness. Great Grandmother's garden was now as neat and colourful as when she had left it, and in the distance the forest trees had grown taller and straighter and more healthy.

James looked down at himself. If the house had changed in the last two years, then surely he had changed even more. As soon as he had gone to the Academy, he had started to grow, and now he was taller even than Mark and almost as large as Rory. With special help from a physiotherapist, he was walking better, and his left hand grew stronger each day. He was top of his class and Captain of the school's Junior Archery team, and he had quite forgotten what it was like to feel shy.

He looked across at the forest—his forest—and a

glow of pride spread through him. One day he would go to College and learn all about the care and management of trees, and then he would come home and take over the great inheritance that the Ugly Man had left him. Stuffy office jobs were not for the Brodies of Craigiburn.

An anxious squeaking reminded him then that it would soon be feeding time for the famous champion cavies. The harness-room door stood open, and inside Jamie could see the rows and tiers of neat hutches. Only last week Peter's son, by a great granddaughter of The Emperor, had won the highest award a cavy can win.

James was not the only person in the district who had changed. Gordon had come back after his first term at boarding-school a very different boy. Instead of being the oldest and cleverest boy in a little school, he had become the smallest and stupidest boy in a very large school, and every one of the other seven hundred boys had made it their personal business to 'take him down a peg'.

Each holiday he came home a little nicer than when he had gone away, and Mark often said, "He's really almost human now." He came to kirk and club whenever he could, and he listened to the minister as attentively as everyone else.

Of course, the biggest change of all was ... but someone was calling him from the house. He scrambled down from the tree at once and made for the back door.

Yes, here was the biggest change of all. Round the

table laden with beautiful scones, cakes, jams and buns, sat Father, Mark and the beautiful woman.

"Come on, Jamie," grinned Mark; "I'm starving!"

When Father had said grace, James could not help thinking to himself, "It's a pity she didn't wait a few years, then she could have married me, but I suppose it's better to have Mark as a brother than a stepson!"

Great Grandmother's Bible lay in the place of honour, while the picture of Harry, the black sheep of the family, stood on the mantelpiece. Now that God lived in the lives of the four people sitting round the table, the Brodies of Craigiburn lived in peace once again.